Targeted

Demographics

M000220351

Targeted Demographics

Joseph Sciuto

IGUANA

Copyright © 2018 Joseph Sciuto

Published by Iguana Books
720 Bathurst Street, Suite 303
Toronto, Ontario, Canada
M5S 2R4

All rights reserved. No part of this publication may be reproduced, stored
in a retrieval system or transmitted, in any form or by any means,
electronic, mechanical, recording or otherwise (except brief passages for
purposes of review) without the prior permission of the author or a licence
from The Canadian Copyright Licensing Agency (Access Copyright). For
an Access Copyright licence, visit www.accesscopyright.ca or call toll free
to 1-800-893-5777.

ISBN (paperback): 978-1-77180-271-0
ISBN (EPUB): 978-1-77180-272-7
ISBN (Kindle): 978-1-77180-273-4

Publisher: Mary Ann J. Blair
Cover image: Petrut Romeo Paul/Shutterstock.com
Cover design: Ruth Dwight

This is an original print edition of *Targeted Demographics*.

To my Mother and Father, my Aunt Carmela and Uncle Al

Chapter One

I've been called a marketing guru, an expert, and the very best in the business. I've been behind some of the most successful advertising campaigns over the last decade — boosting sales, respectability, and admiration for auto, pharmaceutical, oil, and tobacco companies, the US Military, the LAPD, and the movie studios. My motto is simple: "It's okay if I know it's a lie, as long as my target audience believes the lie and buys the product." It was a simple maxim to live by, and God, have I made a lot of money.

One night, standing at the bar at the Smokehouse Restaurant in Burbank, California, enjoying a few ice-cold Budweiser beers, I met Nancy and everything changed.

I have struggled to come up with an appropriate way to describe my Nancy — ironic, considering my job is basically to describe the beauty in things. What I can say about Nancy is that she makes Delilah, the biblical vixen — and the one played by the beautiful actress Hedy Lamarr in the movie version of *Samson and Delilah* — look like a Disney mermaid. That's not to say that my Nancy is evil. In truth, Nancy is the most conscientious and faithful individual I've met in LA. Unlike me, she refuses to lie. Nancy's intellect and knowledge are astonishing. She is compassionate, but when she encounters injustice or despicable individuals such as rapists or pedophiles, or people abusing cats or dogs or the elderly, the repercussions can at times be quite literally deadly.

In the end, it was the same old story. Boy meets girl. Boy falls madly in love with girl. Girl turns out to be a mad and deranged scientist.

I was blinded by her radiance, her supreme intellect, sharp, biting, wit, and her passionate loyalty to the underdog, along with an undying belief in truth, justice, and the American way.

Chapter Two

Everything has a beginning, and not all beginnings begin at birth. Some ancient philosopher high on herbal tea and organic mushrooms came up with that tidbit of wisdom. As for my Nancy, I still am not quite sure where it all began, so let me start at the very beginning.

It had been a long day at work. Trying to put a positive spin on smoking cigarettes wasn't easy. Using old clips of Bogart and Bacall lighting up didn't cut it anymore, especially with the Surgeon General coming out with dire warnings all the time. It was time to take the leap across the pond and jump into the Asian market, which was ripe, ready, and willing to imitate everything the West had to offer. Of course, the tobacco company we were representing wasn't ready to give up totally on the good old USA. I was working on what I called "targeted" campaigning — selecting parts of the country where the youth with no future were naturally hungry for a fresh and uplifting habit, something to distract from the downtrodden poverty they were living in. Places like the South Bronx, South Central LA, Appalachia, border towns along the Mexican border with Texas, and lovely, deteriorating Detroit. Also, teenage girls obsessed with their weight. Hungry for a donut? Why not light up instead? No calories!

The campaign was put on hold because the tobacco companies were under pressure from not only the Surgeon General, but also congressional committees and the heart and lung associations. They didn't want to suddenly add fuel to the fire. Our client assured us that in a few months, after everything had blown over, they would be ready to move forward. After all, you wouldn't want some silly things like cancer, heart disease, and shortened life expectancy to get in the way of corporate profits, would you?

I was drinking an ice-cold beer, leaning against the bar at the Smokehouse Restaurant. The Smokehouse was a Hollywood relic; originally the home of Danny Kaye before being sold and converted into the eatery. It was directly across from a major studio and at the foot of Forest Lawn Cemetery, the final resting place of many famous people. At the top of the cemetery is a museum dedicated to the history of our great nation. Large murals outside the museum depict major battles fought during the Revolutionary War, the Civil War, and World War II, honoring the sacrifices of the many men and women responsible for the survival and greatness of our country. Waterfalls and gardens separate the different murals, making the setting an oasis. On slow days at work I would drive up there and drink a few beers in the peace and quiet, imagining the stories buried beneath the tombstones, stories never to be uncovered.

I noticed an unusual energy shift among the patrons at the bar. It was as though the proverbial bright light at the end of the tunnel had suddenly appeared. Everyone — men and women alike — looked up in wonder as if they had just discovered the answer to the mystery of life. A young lady with long, dirty-blonde hair and a killer body sat down a few stools from me. I couldn't see her face because I was standing with my back to the entrance to the bar, but she was undoubtedly the source of the fascinated affection I saw all around me.

She laid down her purse and ordered a glass of the house white wine, then reached into her purse and took out a copy of Joseph Conrad's *Heart of Darkness*. This was shocking because people in Los Angeles were lucky if they knew how to read, much less one of the greatest novels ever written. Before I cashed in my dream of being a famous novelist and went for the easy money in advertising, I always carried a copy of Conrad's book with me.

I quickly assumed what every pig would: *Sure, she's got a killer body and great hair, but I bet the face doesn't match.* It would take at least ten more beers before it all came together. I remarked, "You have wonderful taste in literature." She didn't even lift her head to say, "I know."

I backed off and figured it wasn't worth the trouble. The bitch is so fucked up that she can't even get a date; she had to come to this bar alone and pretend to read a classic, which she probably couldn't comprehend. I had a few more beers and noticed that the other patrons were still looking intently at her, including a group of older men who, with fleeting movements only, signaled that they were still alive.

I couldn't resist trying to get her to turn around. I needed to see her face. "I used to carry that book around with me everywhere I went."

Again without looking up, "Sure you did, and probably Joyce's *A Portrait of an Artist as a Young Man.*"

"You know, you don't have to be rude."

"Sure I do." With this she lifted her head, pushed back her hair, and looked at me with giant round blue eyes. Her complexion was radiant, unlike that of any of the women I knew. She had the face of a Mediterranean goddess, but her accent was distinctly American. "If I'm not at least a little rude, you might get the wrong impression and think you have a chance of getting into my pants."

"The furthest thing from my mind."

She smiled and turned back to reading the book.

"So who do you think Marlow's aunt represents?" It was a question only someone who had read the book more than a few times would ask.

"I think the aunt represents colonial aristocrats who willingly turned their backs on the inhumane and treacherous behavior their government sanctioned under the disguise of progress." She said this bitingly, her anger barely contained.

"Wow! I just thought she was a nice person," I joked.

"Conrad was too brilliant a writer to use the aunt as a prop."

"So, do you see a parallel between *Heart of Darkness* and what is going on in the world today?"

"Except for the mode of transportation Marlow used, there is very little difference. Colonization might not look as horrifying as it did back then, but it isn't any less terrifying, inhumane, and disgusting." She finished her glass of wine, and Fernando, the bartender, asked if she wanted a refill. "No thanks. Unless the guy behind me wants to buy me a drink?"

Fernando looked at me. "Sure, but give her your top-shelf glass of white. Her taste in wine is woefully lacking." She looked back at me and smiled. My heart skipped a beat. She was stunning, and not shy.

"Let me guess, a woefully overpaid producer?"

"No!"

"A wannabe gangster with no connections?" Now she was just having fun with me.

"Nope. And you? A Beverly Hills bitch that's never passed a mirror you didn't fall in love with? What were you thinking with that trashy house wine? Did daddy disinherit you?"

She looked across at me, then reached over and touched my sport coat. "Armani, my favorite. Can I wear it? It's chilly in here."

"I'll ask them to turn off the air conditioner."

"Afraid I might walk out with it?"

Fernando placed the wine down in front of her. She picked it up, said "Cheers," took a large gulp and swirled it around in her mouth. Then pretended to choke and spit it up all over me, exclaiming, "Disgusting!"

I was covered in wine. "You did that on purpose! What the hell?"

She calmly grabbed a couple of napkins and wiped me off.

"Why on earth would you do that?"

"I figured it was the only way to get the jacket off you. Forgive me?"

"No!"

"Please?" She took a small sip of the wine, swished it around her mouth again, and swallowed. "Delicious. Wonderful choice."

I took my wine-drenched jacket off and put it over her shoulders.

"Thank you. I promise I don't have any germs or terrible diseases that I know about."

"You can have it. The jacket, I mean."

"Thanks." She *seemed* indifferent, but this woman was full of surprises.

I started toward the bathroom to clean up and she called after me, "I'll be right here waiting for you."

After I came back, we had a few more drinks at the bar, ate dinner, had a few more drinks at the bar, and then went back to my place. We had a few more drinks while listening to Ol' Blue Eyes. We then made it into my bedroom, ripped our clothes off, and made love; or at least that's what I imagined.

When I woke up the next morning she was gone. I searched the house like a child searching for a favorite toy. The only thing left was the scent of her perfume. No note or phone number. Nothing.

Required Reading: *Introduction 101, The Genesis of Nancy.*

Chapter Three

Work was difficult, but in the end very satisfying. The tobacco company was overjoyed with my targeting strategy. The campaign might be on hold, but the ideas kept on coming. I felt like an armchair general, decoding and identifying the enemy's weaknesses and exploiting them to the max. Urban teenagers looking for an escape, disregarding the Surgeon General's warning on each pack. Once hooked, customers for life — an abbreviated life, but nobody's allowed all the cookies in the jar. The Asian market, a billion or more potential lifetime customers, tariffs or no tariffs — a win-win situation: Build the factories there, employ their people at one-third the wages of American workers — fewer tariffs, more profits.

I was feeling good about myself as I walked into the Smokehouse. The bar, like always, was half full of the same old patrons. The first few beers went down easily, and then I noticed a few people's eyes shift to the entrance. I could smell her before I saw her. She wore such a lovely scent. She sat down next to me wearing my Armani jacket; or should I say *her* Armani jacket?

"Did you miss me?" she asked lustily. I ordered her a wine.

"You could have left me a note."

"I knew you would be back here tonight."

"Still…"

"I didn't take you for the insecure type, Joe."

"How did you get home?

"I called a cab, which reminds me, I borrowed fifty dollars out of your wallet. You had a whole stack of them. I figured you wouldn't mind. I didn't want to wake you."

"A fifty-dollar cab ride? Do you live that far away?"

"No, less than a mile, but I left a really good tip and used the rest of the money to buy lunch."

I touched her jacket as she reached over and grabbed the wine.

"I see you had the jacket cleaned."

"The wardrobe department at the studio. They love doing favors for me."

"Why did you choose makeup? You could be on the cover of half the fashion magazines in the country, not to mention overseas."

"I love chemicals. I get to play on the supposed prettiest faces in the world. So where are we going to eat tonight?"

"Wherever you like." She looked at me deviously.

"Or we can just go back to your place, order in, drink some wine, listen to some music, and get naughty."

Her suggestion sounded wonderful, but I balked at the idea. "I think I would rather eat out."

"Great! So tell me, Joseph, what is your line of work?"

"I put together advertising campaigns for companies."

"For what type of companies?"

"All types … entertainment, fashion, beverage, liquor, oil and gas."

"Sounds exciting and quite lucrative."

"Yes, it is."

"Care to share? Any companies I might know?"

"I'm not at liberty to share that information." I lied, but I saw this going in a direction I didn't like, and I wasn't about to lose this precious jewel over some stupid questions about morals.

She laughed. "Is that the best you can come up with?"

"It's the truth."

"If you say so, Joey." She squeezed my cheek as if I were a toddler. "Billboards, commercials, radio spots, ads in magazines, table tents?" She picked up a table tent off the bar. It featured a list of premium drinks.

"Nothing like that, but little things like table tents can do a business a lot of good without costing a fortune."

"I'm sure, but stuff like that is child's play for someone with your intellect and lifestyle. A handful of corporations control what we see, what we eat, what bad habits we pick up, and what we want to look like when we look in the mirror. It's people like you who promote their lies."

"If you say so, Nancy."

"Don't get angry, Joe. I apply makeup to a bunch of talentless assholes that need to read cue cards because they're incapable of memorizing anything more than a few lines. I'm starving; is it okay if we just eat here?"

The hostess sat us at a table toward the back of the restaurant. Nancy playfully put out her hands, revealing that the jacket sleeves were way too long. "It fits perfectly except for the sleeves. That will be the next thing I have the wardrobe department do. I wouldn't want anyone to think I stole it off the rack."

I looked at her and tried to remember what she looked like naked. "The end of last night is a little blurry."

"Not to worry, you didn't do anything astounding. You only lasted a few moments. The cleanup took longer than the limited sparks between us."

I was speechless. I didn't know if I was just embarrassed, or if it was the detached and dispassionate way she delivered her critique. It was like I had been slapped.

She touched my hand. "Don't you worry, Joe. I'm sure you'll do better tonight."

I pretended to read the menu, my head buried between the pages.

"I think I'm going to have the fillet," she said. "Is it any good?"

"Yes, it's their best steak."

The waitress took our order and I tried to regain my composure.

"So, where are you from, Nancy?"

"Surely, Joe, an advertising guru like yourself should be able to figure that out in your sleep."

"What, did you talk to the publicity department at the studio?"

"Yes, they were quite forthcoming with all kinds of praise for you. I think a couple of the girls over there have the hots for you. If it doesn't work out between us, although I don't see any reason why it won't, I think you would be wise to check out those girls."

"That's a real backhanded suggestion on your part."

"A girl can't be too careful these days. Don't be so sensitive. I thought boys from the Bronx were supposed to be tough."

"You're an amazing piece of work."

"I know! I've been told that many times ... Oh, I almost forgot," She reached down into her purse and took out a copy of *Heart of Darkness* and *A Portrait of the Artist as a Young Man*. She handed me the books that were in really bad shape and filled with hundreds of notes in the margins.

"I already own a couple of copies of both these books."

"But not with my notes and analysis in the margins. I think you would greatly appreciate my insights and get a better and fuller understanding of both books if you read what I wrote."

I flipped through the pages of both books and I swear there were more of her words in the margins than there were words in either book. "What, did you do a thesis on these books?"

"No, silly, I just like taking notes."

"Maybe you should intern as a book editor. I could help you get started. I have a number of connections in the publishing world."

"That's sweet, but I have much bigger plans."

She picked up a piece of bread and neatly spread butter across it. She slowly ate a tiny amount as she looked across at me. "So tell me, do you ever plan on being the novelist you dreamt of being before you sold your soul to the corporate world?"

"How do you even know that I ever wanted to be a novelist?"

"It's an easy deduction. No one who has such a marvelous collection of books doesn't dream one day of writing a great novel. Before I left your place I took a tour of your library."

"And let me guess, you have read all the books in my library?"

"Not all, but most. I haven't ventured nearly as far as you have into the Russian novelists. Maybe when I get a little time, if you don't mind me marking up your books, I'll get around to reading them."

"Just tell me when you're ready and I will gladly buy you the books."

"Don't like people messing around with your books?"

"Exactly!"

"Okay, I will make you a list and you can buy them for me. Penguin is my preferred publisher when it comes to translations."

She put another piece of bread in her mouth. "I bet you have some great stories about growing up in the Bronx. You should write them down before you get too old and forget them."

"I don't expect my memory to go anytime soon. At least, I hope not."

"You can never be too vigilant."

"Is that why you write down every thought you have?"

"Not every thought, Joseph, just the important ones."

"Can you please not call me Joseph? My mother used to call me Joseph when I was in trouble. It feels disrespectful to her memory."

"I didn't mean any disrespect."

"I know you didn't. How could you possibly know that my mother used to call me Joseph when I misbehaved?"

The waitress brought our food and we ordered more drinks. After dinner we went back over to the bar and drank some more, then went back to my place, listened to Duke Ellington, and after more drinks we were finally in my bedroom, taking off each other's clothes. I was determined not to have a repeat of last night. I didn't care what it took, but it couldn't be thirty seconds and out. All those tricks like thinking about God and damnation didn't work, at least not for me. I would take the safest course, extended foreplay. Kiss, lick, bury my head between her breasts, but keep that brainless prick out of the greatest source of pleasure for as long as possible.

We kissed for what seemed like an eternity but it was probably about a minute. I moved slowly down her body, kissing and licking what seemed like every inch of her, whispering sweet nothings in her ear. She seemed unusually quiet, but I didn't think anything of it, at least not at first. Around her breasts, I started to feel a little uneasy. I figured I would at least get some sort of moan or groan from her, but she was silent. I looked up and saw her eyes closed, which wasn't so unusual, but her breathing was steady, no panting or puffing. She resembled a kitten asleep, and as it turned out that's exactly what she was ... asleep!

Last night's critique was tough enough to hear, but this was downright insulting. It's not like I ever considered myself a Casanova, but this made me feel like a young, inexperienced boy. Like I was having an out-of-body experience. I thought of waking her, but that would make me look like a pathetic fool — or continuing with the downward progression and finishing what we had started, but that made me feel like some sort of rapist. I rolled over, closed my eyes, and quietly wept as my manhood was once again diminished.

She was gone the following morning by the time I woke up. It was eerie she was so quiet that she never disturbed me. Then again, I didn't know what time she left. I did a short search of the house to make sure she was really gone then showered and got ready for work. I picked up my wallet off the kitchen table and found a note. She thanked me for a wonderful night and listed about thirty Russian novels that I had promised to get her. Many of the names I'd never heard of and pronouncing their names was out of the question. She said it was no rush, but she would greatly appreciate it if I could get them as quickly as possible. She borrowed another fifty dollars, which meant that she owed me a hundred. She said she hoped I wasn't charging interest, because there was a real good chance that it might take her a long time to pay me back. She left her work phone number and said I could call her anytime, even if it was to just hear her voice. She signed the note with a *love you*. I folded the paper and stuffed it in the inside pocket of my suit jacket.

Chapter Four

I sat on the edge of Maggie's desk. She was my faithful and trusted assistant, who had been with me for years. We had an easy relationship. She understood me, and, even though we were professional colleagues, we were also friends. We confided in each other and sort of looked after each other.

Born and raised in southern California, Maggie was a traditional girl for her time. She had a killer body, a lovely face, and was able to wiggle her nose like Elizabeth Montgomery on *Bewitched*. We had a number of wild nights back when we first started working together, which usually ended with us stretched out on my office couch, half-naked and stinking from liquor, marijuana, and sex. Before I had a chance to seriously fall for her she married some rich guy, popped out a couple of children, got divorced, married a different rich guy, got divorced again — and all of this before she was thirty. She never lost the killer body, but she had lost some of the shine in her eyes. Maggie was the one person I could talk to and trust that it wouldn't become office gossip.

I was getting ready to talk to her about Nancy when a pang of embarrassment and male vanity got in the way of my confession.

"What is it, Joe?" she asked a few times before I shook my head and mumbled, "Nothing. It's nothing at all."

Maggie informed me that Jack had called a meeting for ten o'clock in the conference room. Jack was the owner of the firm and every month or so he would call a meeting during which nothing of any importance was ever discussed. He had to remind the rest of us that he was an active player in the business.

I handed Maggie the list of books Nancy wanted and asked if she would call the local bookstores to see if, by some miracle, they stocked the books on the list. She could go pick the books up after lunch, drop them off, and take the rest of the day off. I gave her my credit card and told her to buy something nice for the kids and herself as a perk.

I went into my office and looked at the notes on the whiteboard for a media blitz aimed at specific targets. "Cool is lighting a cute girl's cigarette before she has a chance to light it herself." "Cool is lighting up after intensely satisfying sex."

Maggie knocked on the door and handed me a message. "Nancy. She says it's urgent." I crumbled the piece of paper and flipped it into the trash. Maggie stood by, wiggling her cute nose and smiling.

"Don't you have work to do?" I asked.

"Yeah, but it can wait." She sat on the edge of my desk and crossed her legs in a seductive manner. "Just weighing my options now that I'm single again."

"Is that so?"

"Nancy seemed a little unhinged, to put it mildly. Before plunging into that nightmare, you might want to look at a more stable and reliable choice…"

"And is that choice you?"

"It could be. We did have a really good thing going for a while."

"Yeah, and then you ran off and got married, popped out a few kids, got divorced, got married again…"

"Okay, I don't need a thorough rehashing of my bad choices. A girl has to secure her future before it overtakes her. But my future at the moment is fairly stable." She reached over and kissed me, and I instinctively kissed her back. "You see, the sparks are still there." She winked and started walking toward the door. "Just something to think about, Joe." She closed the door behind her and I looked back at the board. Suddenly I wished for a cigarette, and I didn't even smoke.

I waited a few minutes before calling Nancy. I could feel Maggie's eyes on me and I didn't want her to think that Nancy had gotten under my skin, even though that had definitely happened. Maybe Nancy had discovered a pill that cured the disease she was suffering from. Bitch-a-cillin? One could only hope.

I finally returned her call. "Is everything okay?"

"Yes, I just wanted to add two more books to the list."

"That's what was urgent?"

"I'm a fanatic when it comes to details. Who was the dimwit who answered the phone?"

I didn't reply. Maggie, above all else, was my closest friend.

"Are you fucking her?" Nancy asked derisively. I took a deep breath and replied harshly, "Don't call back." I hung up the phone determined to hold my ground.

I called Maggie back into the office and told her to forget about ordering the books. I sat down on the couch and looked across at the board as Maggie sat beside me. "Trouble in paradise?" she asked.

"Nothing that can't be fixed simply enough." I continued to look at the board as she comfortably leaned back. "Maggie, do you ever think that what we do here is totally immoral?"

"We're not breaking any laws, and if we don't do it some other firm will."

"What I have up there is targeting young Blacks and Latinos already born with two strikes against them. How would you feel if I was targeting your children with an addictive substance that would eventually cut their lives short?"

"How about we go out tonight for a few drinks and dinner? We haven't done that in a long time. I just have to be home by eight to tuck the kids in."

"That would be great. Make a reservation. Any place but the Smokehouse."

She got up and looked down at me, "Do I still get to take off after lunch and buy myself and the kids something?"

"I don't see why not. How about we meet in the lobby at f.

"Sounds great! Thank you, Joe." She blew me a kiss and for sᴏ reason I couldn't help sensing that Maggie was stoned. Her eyes looked cloudy, and she seemed strangely disconnected. I shook my head and figured it was just Nancy inside my head.

The top-level executives — nine men and one woman — sat around the conference table. Some brought pads and pens with them just to look good, not for a moment expecting anything out of our fearless leader's mouth to be worth writing down. Jack entered the room pulling up his pants and muttering something incomprehensible. He was medium height, balding, quite affable, and always unkempt. He was proud of the work we were all doing and the company was on sound financial footing. He envisioned the firm expanding to Chicago and New York and eventually to the United Kingdom. He had been saying that for the last six years while the only thing expanding was his waistline with each new divorce. The truth was there was no need to expand. Business came to us from throughout the United States and overseas and with all the technological advances, most of our business was handled through video conference calls.

I imagine Jack saw himself as another JP Morgan. He had started the company over thirty years ago and for the longest time he bowed to no one. He was behind some of the most successful advertising bonanzas in history, making housewives swoon over the latest kitchen and household appliances. University classes were taught based solely on Jack's techniques, but the good life eventually got to him — too much virgin pussy, coke, booze, and a string of nasty divorces, but, unlike other successful businessmen brought down by their vices, Jack was smart enough to hire the very best person in the advertising world to pick up the slack. He hired me, and the company was doing better than ever. Sadly, a sizable chunk of seaside property along the California coast was being handed over in each divorce settlement.

The meeting ended on a high note with Jack chanting, "We are the champions! We are the champions!" It was quite moving except for the fact that he'd forgotten to zip up his pants that morning. And since Jack wasn't wearing any underwear, we all got a firsthand look at something *National Geographic* would have censored.

I made it all the way to the door of the conference room before Jack put a hand on my shoulder and led me into his office. He closed the door, took out two glasses and a bottle of thirty-six-year-old scotch, and poured us each a double.

"To pussy, my boy. To pussy!" He toasted and quickly refilled our glasses.

"Heard you were seen having dinner with a knockout blonde two nights in a row."

"Yeah, but it's not going any further than it has," I replied as I tried to get a handle on the situation.

"Yeah, that's what I originally said about every bitch I eventually married. It's not going any further." He raised his glass and we toasted again and shot down the doubles.

"Recently, I discovered a treasure trove of pussy that won't cost you every hard-earned dollar you make. The best I've ever had and such variety you can't even imagine." Jack reached down into his desk and took out a photo album and handed it to me. "Go ahead, open it. Discover what every successful man can have without the shackles of a marriage license attached."

I opened the book and looked down at a variety of young beautiful girls: Russian, Spanish, Asian, Latina, Italian, and American.

"Niiice, right?" Jack delightfully remarked.

"Very nice. What are they, high-class hookers?"

"Not just high-class hookers, the very best. Not just beautiful, but really smart. A couple of nights ago I had an English fox reciting Shakespeare for me while she was riding my cock. Didn't understand a word she was saying, but God did it turn me on. What you have in front of you, Joe, is the answer to all your problems with women. Fuck and forget, fuck and forget … no strings attached. A thousand a night and whatever else you might want to throw in, like dinner and drinks before you get down to the serious business. Variety galore. I mean, look at those babes. Who needs a nagging wife — who in the end is going to take you for everything — when a simple grand a night will satisfy your needs without the worry of having to satisfy *her* needs?"

"I must admit it makes sense, Jack. And in the long run it'll save you a fortune."

"I'm not trying to tell you what to do, Joe, but I don't want you to fall victim to the same shit as I've been, over and over. Love is a load of crap women thought up to shackle us and drain every last ounce of a man's dignity and hard-earned cash."

"This last divorce really hurt, huh?"

"They all hurt, but this one seriously made me realize what a sucker I've been. I could own half of Malibu if it wasn't for these greedy broads I married, who never contributed a fucking penny and walked away with fortunes. You've been such an asset to this company, Joe. Your first ten girls are on me."

"No, Jack. I wouldn't feel right about that."

"Don't worry about feeling right. I know you're one of those literary guys who actually reads books. Maybe that English girl I was with a couple of nights ago is available."

"No, not the English chick. I mean, nothing against English women, but they're so pasty it's as though they don't have blood running through their bodies."

"I never thought about that, but you're right. She was in serious need of a spray tan, but I was so turned on with her athleticism that I really didn't notice. She did a 360 while riding my cock!"

"Holy shit! That is amazing."

"I ejaculated so hard she actually fell backward. But the best are the Russian chicks, so young and pure looking; for an extra hundred on the side they'll let you explore every inch of their bodies. Last night I had a Russian and I can still smell her scent all over me. My dick felt like a little Marco Polo, discovering new worlds, entering the heart of darkness while my hand played with her pussy and the other hand cupped her voluptuous tits. A little dirty, I admit, but nothing a little soap and water didn't wash away."

I felt the shots of scotch coming back up and immediately reached for a beer and downed it.

"Are you okay?" Jack asked.

"Yeah! Just needed something to cool the fever in my mouth."

We had a couple more shots and a few beers and then I left his office. He insisted that I take the album with me. He already had the whole weekend planned and paid for, one hundred percent Russian. He said he wouldn't mind if I wanted to come over to his place for a little sample. The girls wouldn't mind; it's extra cash for them. I told him I was planning on working the whole weekend, but I really appreciated the invitation and would give it some thought.

I stumbled back to my office. Maggie was already gone. She must have decided that since she had the afternoon off she might as well take an early lunch. She'd left a note on my desk that read, "She called eleven times! Urgent! Good luck. See you at five."

Chapter Five

I took my jacket off and fell facedown onto the couch. I woke up at four-thirty and looked out my office window to find that everyone was already gone. On Fridays, everyone left at four and went down to the bar at Mo's Restaurant, a couple of buildings over. I took a bottle of mouthwash and a toothbrush and toothpaste out of my desk and walked to the bathroom. I threw cold water on my face and rinsed and cleaned my mouth for an extended period of time. Considering that the only thing I'd had all day was four shots of scotch and a few beers, I was feeling fairly well.

I walked back to my office and thought I heard laughing down the hall. I didn't think anything of it and placed my things with Jack's album into my desk. When I put on my jacket and walked back out, the laughter continued. It was women's laughter and it was coming from Jack's office. I couldn't help myself as I slowly walked toward his door. It was closed but I could easily see in through the slits in the blinds. Three dark-haired beauties no older than twenty-two danced around Jack dressed in traditional Russian Khokhloma dresses and Siberian hats. Jack was lying naked on his desk with an unlit cigar in his mouth and a bottle of scotch beside him. The girls would occasionally stop, all at once, and pull up the front of their dresses and then turn and wiggle their naked butts in Jack's face.

I got onto the elevator, trying to process what I had just seen. At the lobby, I saw Maggie flirting with five different guys at the front desk. She was dressed to kill with high platform heels, a short skirt, and a cut-off white T-shirt that left little to the imagination. If I didn't know better, I would have thought she was the second act after Jack was finished with the three Russians.

She threw her hands around my neck and kissed me like she was trying to suck the life out of me. The piece of gum she was chewing got attached to my teeth. I detached the gum and put it back in her mouth. We walked to my car and she nearly tripped a half-dozen times. I bent down and took off her high heels. She suddenly was eight inches shorter and I got the pleasure of holding her high heels until we got to the car.

I drove out of the parking lot and asked, "What, did you smoke a whole field of weed?"

"Not the whole field, but maybe half." She laughed and her nose wiggled.

"You reek of the shit."

"Is it really that bad?" She took out a bottle of perfume and was about to spray herself when I stopped her.

"That won't do a thing except make it worse. Please, tell me you haven't been driving in your condition?"

"No! I took a limo. You're always telling me I have to watch out for myself. I took your advice. The bill will show up on your next credit card statement, and yes, I left a really good tip like you always do."

"Did you actually go shopping?"

"Of course I did. I bought a bunch of wonderful things."

"Wonderful in that they cost a lot?"

"Wonderful does come at a price, Joe. Surely, if anyone knows that it's you."

"Let me guess … $5,000?" She tried to calculate using her fingers.

"A little bit more, but that includes the limo." She handed my credit card back to me.

I stopped at a red light and looked at her. She was stoned, relaxed, smiling, and adorable. Maggie didn't have a mean-spirited bone in her body. She was familiar and comfortable. I reached over and kissed her affectionately on top of her head. "I love you, Maggie."

"I love you too, Joe."

I parked the car in the lot behind the Monte Carlo Restaurant and Deli. I grabbed a pair of sneakers out of the trunk of the car and Maggie put them on. She objected at first but I told her the only one she had to impress was me and she had already done that. The sneakers were way too big on her, but it was better that customers thought of her as a homeless beauty than a high-class hooker. Monte Carlo was famous for its Italian food and pastries. The deli section was as big, if not bigger, than the famous Carnegie Deli in New York.

We sat at a small table by the window, and before the waiter could say hello or take our drink order, Maggie ordered three cannoli and then another. Our drinks arrived and Maggie scrutinized the menu like an actor trying to remember her lines. She drank her glass of red wine in a matter of seconds. I ordered a bottle and as the waiter was uncorking it, Maggie was ordering lasagna, ravioli, and a meatball hero. She didn't wait for him to finish pouring the wine before she grabbed her glass. Wine went all over the place but not before Maggie downed what the waiter had managed to pour. It was like watching a Marx Brothers' movie.

I finally got her to settle down. In all the years I'd known her, I'd never seen Maggie like this, not that I could recall. She was drawing attention from other diners and the staff for all the wrong reasons.

At Maggie's insistence, the waiter brought the food quickly. Her three entrees very likely weighed more than she did. I had a meatball hero, which I ate quickly because I expected at any moment that she might snatch it out of my hand and scarf it down. She slowed down over time and actually waited for the waiter to finish filling her next glass before sipping.

She suddenly stopped everything — eating, drinking, talking — and looked at me as though for the first time. It was like she had awakened from a trance and found herself in an unfamiliar place. "I have an important question to ask you. Will you please answer it honestly?"

"Okay."

"If I didn't run off and marry my loser first husband, would you have eventually asked me to marry you? Be honest, Joe."

The answer to her question was yes, but I wasn't sure that was what she wanted to hear. From the moment I saw Maggie I was attracted to her, and after several wild nights together I had fallen for her deeply. She was not only very attractive but had an infectious and carefree personality that made me feel an ease I rarely found with anyone else. Of course it was risky because we worked together, so I told myself it was casual fun and neither of us was taking it too seriously. We didn't have much in common. I loved classic literature while Maggie enjoyed fashion and entertainment magazines. Her extensive knowledge on both subjects made my job a lot easier. She was often the key advisor I confided in before making a presentation, and her insights and perceptions were always right on the mark. She had wonderful taste and a natural understanding of what women wanted and desired, making her a tremendous asset to the work. She could decipher a bullshit and condescending ad and fix it easily, like a great film editor.

Well, she did say honestly, so I replied, "Yes, Maggie. I would have married you."

Sadly, that was the wrong answer. After a moment's reflection, she threw her hands straight up in the air and brought them crashing down on the table as she buried her head into the plate of lasagna and started to cry. Her sobbing was uncontrollable, and very loud. The meltdown progressed with plates and glasses flying everywhere. Thankfully, I was able to grab my glass of wine and the bottle before they hit the floor.

For the longest moment, it was like the place had gone silent except for Maggie's wailing, and it wasn't like they were looking exclusively at her but at me, as if I was surely the cause of her tantrum. I calmly sipped the wine or pretended to. Waiters and other employees ran over to the table, asking if she was all right as they hastily tried to clean up the mess.

I tried to put a reassuring hand on her, and she picked up a knife, screaming, "Don't you dare!"

I handed out about $1000 to the staff in appreciation for their help and concern and ordered another bottle of wine. I reassured them that Maggie was fine. She was a little depressed about failing her driver's test for the fourth time. I stared at her as the sobbing went on nonstop and the one thought I could not shake from my mind was, *I truly hope that dish of lasagna didn't do any damage to that wonderful little nose.*

She finally did lift her head, and her face and hair and clothes were covered with tomato sauce. There was a time not too long ago when the thought of licking all that sauce off her would have been a real turn-on, but it wasn't now. I quickly checked the table for any sharp objects; there weren't any. Then I grabbed the bottle of wine. I had already spent a small fortune on Maggie that day and I wasn't in the mood to have to order another bottle. Thankfully, her nose looked intact as she said to me, "I have to go to the bathroom and pee." She walked away holding her crotch like a toddler.

She was gone for a long time. I was reluctant to ask a waitress or the hostess to go check on her. After all, why cut their lives short because the lunatic in the bathroom got a bad bag of weed? I didn't care how stoned she was — something was definitely not right. Whatever she smoked was laced with something or tainted somehow. This behavior was outrageous.

I seriously dreaded going down to check on her, but that evening Maggie was my responsibility. She was my one true friend, she had two kids at home, and if past circumstances had been just a little different, she might very well have become my wife. Thankfully, she came back all cleaned up and under control. She sat down and, leaning toward me, informed me that she hadn't been able get her panties down quick enough and peed all over them, so she deposited them in the trash. She asked the waiter for a clean glass because she wanted to have more wine. I would have objected, but she was calm for the moment and I didn't want to set her off again.

It was as though nothing had happened. We went on with our meal, and she kept alluding to a certain something she had in store for me at the end of the night. "A little thank you."

I held on to her as we finally left the restaurant and she stumbled to my car. I buckled her in and she whispered something truly disgusting about the "something special" she had planned. She passed out about fifteen seconds later.

I pulled into her driveway in the beautiful Brentwood section of Los Angeles. She had no doubt done very well for herself in the two divorce settlements. I carried the sleeping beauty into the house and was greeted by the nanny and Maggie's two obnoxious children, who were playing Cowboys and Indians. They sprayed their mommy with water from their toy guns but it didn't wake her up. I tucked her into bed as the children screamed. The nanny looked at me as though I was a criminal. She asked in Spanish about the sauce all over Maggie's blouse, thinking it was blood and ready to call the police. It took me a whole half hour to explain the sauce. She nodded unconvincingly and then took out a clean blanket and an extra pillow, assuming I was staying the night. I slowly backed out of the room, saying, "No. No. No!"

Once I made it back to my car, I drove down Sunset Boulevard, passing Bel-Air, Westwood Village, and Beverly Hills, then onto Coldwater Canyon. I had a lot to digest. The same questions I'd been asking myself for the last seven years kept badgering me: What was I doing here in a place so different from the Bronx where I grew up? Was I simply killing time, or would I let myself settle down? Was it finally time to call Los Angeles home?

My parents died just a few weeks apart, shortly after I graduated college. Since then, I carried around a certain amount of guilt that I was responsible for their deaths. My parents would say it was nonsense, but the guilt has persisted.

My parents were Italian and Catholic — more Catholic than Italian. God bless their souls, I don't think either of them spoke a word of Italian. They both worked at a factory called American Banknote, which was located in the crime-ridden neighborhood of Hunts Point in the Bronx. My father was a paper handler while my mom worked on the clerical side. They made a decent living, never missed an opportunity to work overtime, and made sure I attended Catholic schools right through high school. I got into John Jay College of Criminal Justice, which must have been a mistake because my grades were in no way good enough to get accepted.

I made the most of the opportunity, took a full schedule of classes my first semester, and while lingering in the library between classes I accidently picked up a copy of Dostoevsky's *Crime and Punishment*. I started reading it and was hooked, finishing the book in no time. It was probably the first book I ever truly read. Even through twelve years of Catholic school I am fairly confident I never read an entire book. Over the next few months I read the collective works of this master, many of which were over 800 pages. The amazing thing was that none of those titles were assigned to me; I read them on my own while taking a full load of other courses, which I aced. It was as though a totally unused part of my brain had suddenly been awakened. Knowledge had become a new and fascinating high.

After completing my first year at John Jay I transferred to Stony Brook University, which had a highly distinguished English department. It was the first time I lived away from home and my parents weren't thrilled. Italians find it very difficult to understand why any of their children would ever want to leave home unless they're getting married. I was an only child and this made it equally difficult for them. The more I think about it, the more I believe I was the reason for their early demise. I left them and broke their hearts. Nancy is the penance I am paying for my disloyalty.

Chapter Six

I pulled into my driveway and parked. A comfortable bed was waiting for me and maybe a couple more glasses of wine. That would be a wonderful close to the day.

Boy, was I wrong once again! I opened the door and found what just a few days ago would have been the most amazing hallucination, but tonight was another bizarre event. Nancy, wearing panties, a bra, and an Armani sport coat, lay across my couch reading a book that she was — naturally — marking up. I walked slowly toward her as she looked up. "Did you break into my house?"

"I wouldn't exactly call it a break-in. I used the spare key that you keep under the third flower pot to the right of the door."

"And how would you know that I keep a key under that flower pot?"

"Because you think in threes. All of your books are arranged in stacks of three, as are all of your jackets."

"Is that another one of my jackets that you're wearing?"

"Yes, the one you gave me is in the wardrobe department at work. Remember, I'm having them fix the sleeves?"

"What are you doing here, Nancy?"

"Well, when you didn't show up for our dinner date I got worried."

"We didn't have a dinner date."

"I'm sorry, I simply assumed we were having dinner like we did the last two nights. My mistake! But it appears you got a better offer."

I reached down and grabbed her glass of wine. I took a long sip as I looked down at Dostoevsky's *Crime and Punishment*.

"What did I tell you about marking up my books?"

She lifted the book and replied, "This is *my* book. I bought it with the money I borrowed from you this morning. I guess that promise to buy me all the Russian novels I asked for is no longer on the table."

"You guessed right."

"For what it's worth, I'm sorry for calling your assistant a dimwit and assuming that you were fucking her. I didn't realize how much Maggie means to you. It's kind of sweet."

"You're treading on very thin ice, Nancy. You might want to drop it before I kick your sorry little ass out into the street."

"Is that so?" She smiled wickedly, looking at me as though she were ready to dissect and discard me, one body part at a time.

She left me speechless, challenging me with her gaze, taking the wine glass back from my hand. "I think maybe you've already had a little too much wine tonight, hmm?" She picked up the book and started to read and jot notes again.

"Seriously, Nancy, you insult my friend, break into my house, and now you're trying to judge how much I've had to drink?"

"You invited me into your house and into your bed. Surely your memory isn't that bad?"

"What type of lunatic are you?"

She put down the book. "I'm going to let that one slide. The ill-advised words of a guy who's had too much to drink."

"Maybe I should call the cops to have you removed from my property."

"Why don't you do that, Joe? I'll be interested to see how it all ends."

This was getting totally out of control. I took a deep breath, walked into the kitchen, and took out a bottle of chardonnay. I opened the bottle and grabbed two glasses. I poured a glass and put it in front of Nancy, then sat down on the couch, poured myself some, and said, "How about we call a truce? I've had a tough day."

"Of course you have, Joe. It's not easy for a man who has a conscience like yours to do the work you do."

I didn't even bother to reply because that would only open another vein and I had already bled enough for one day. "A truce!"

We tapped glasses; she took a sip and gave me that look again, as though she were about to carve me up. "Thank you, Joe."

She went back to reading her book and I stared up at the ceiling. I just wanted this day to be done. First, Nancy the psycho had ignited the whole thing with the Russian novelists; she was still sitting right beside me. Jack had thrown gasoline on the flame and etched images into my mind that no one should ever have to see. Maggie, usually my safeguard against insanity, had become completely unhinged, threatened me with a knife, cost me thousands, and put me through fifteen minutes of torture as she slept with her adorable nose buried in a dish of lasagna. And now, for the finale, the psychotic bitch who started the whole nightmare was finishing it off in grand fashion.

Nancy put her book down, reached into her sport coat, and took out my spare house key. She placed it in my hand. I asked, "You don't want to hold onto it?"

"No, I can pick any lock in this house in less than thirty seconds. Oh, for the record, your alarm system is childish. A novice criminal could get past it with no problem."

"That's reassuring. Any suggestions?"

"Yeah, two German shepherds."

"Why two?"

"So they can keep each other company. On nights when you and your precious Maggie are out gallivanting around town, and I can't make it over, the dogs will at least have each other. I recommend getting two puppies from the same litter."

She sipped her wine and stared out into nothingness. I didn't even want to imagine what was going on in her mind.

"I need to pee." She put her glass down and walked off to the bathroom. I felt like a prisoner in my own home, held captive by a beautiful sadist whose unpredictability made her all the more frightening and, dare I say, terribly interesting and desirable.

She returned and sat down next to me. "Please don't be mad at me, Joe." At first I thought I heard the wrong words come out of her mouth. Her passions and emotions seemed to be all over the place. She threw her hands tightly around my waist and buried her head in my chest. "Please," she repeated as I stroked her hair.

We fell asleep like that, and when I woke up at five in the morning she was — naturally — gone. My wallet was on the table next to the couch. I picked it up and found a note inside. *I had to borrow a hundred dollars. I now owe you two hundred dollars. Will see you soon. Love, Nancy*

I picked up the dirty glasses and empty wine bottle and walked into the kitchen. I washed the glasses and then took out the garbage. I desperately needed a shower and shave. I let the water run down my body for a long time. I shampooed my hair three times and scrubbed my body with soap but still felt the dirt of yesterday lingering on me.

I got dressed and walked into the living room, just in time to welcome Nancy back into the house. She was carrying a bag and a cup of coffee, smiling as she handed them to me. She had bought me breakfast: French toast with two slices of bacon. That was my favorite breakfast and the coffee was definitely needed. I didn't bother to ask her how she knew what to get me. She would only tell me it was by deduction. She loved that word.

I sat down at the table looking out to the pool, and Nancy sat down beside me. She cupped her hand under her chin and looked at me as if for the first time. It made me uncomfortable, and I started thinking she might have poisoned the food. She could be ready to jot down, in minute detail, every second of my demise. I hesitated before taking a bite. "Didn't you get something for yourself?"

"I had a muffin while waiting for your order."

"Would you like a bite?"

"No! It's for you."

"Are you sure?"

"Don't be silly, Joe." With that she took off my sport coat and revealed a two-piece black bathing suit that almost made me choke on my first bite of French toast.

"Do you like?"

"What's not to like? One would have to be blind, a corpse, or a flaming fag not to like it."

"Thank you. I'm so happy you have a pool. I love to swim but find it uncomfortable swimming at the gym I belong to. Just a bunch of perverts staring at me like I'm a piece of meat."

"How about swimming in the ocean?"

"Even worse; a bunch of surfer dudes with the IQ of donkeys making lewd and insulting remarks."

"I see how it can be tough."

"Evolution came to a halt for men about a thousand years ago, when you started thinking solely with your penises."

"Very good French toast..." I desperately tried to change the subject. It did not escape me that she included me with all the other men in mentioning the evolution of the male species.

"Does it taste as good as what your father would make for you on Saturday mornings?"

"Almost, but not quite." I was ready to ask how she knew my father made French toast on Saturday mornings, and then I remembered — simple deduction.

Chapter Seven

She walked outside, tucked her hair under a swimming cap, and dove into the pool with barely a splash, and like a teenage boy I waited for her top to come loose and float off. She was right; I was thinking with my penis. I was a perfect example of the stalled evolution of the male species. A thousand years of thinking solely with our genitals.

I cleared the table as the coffee gave me that much-needed boost. A Japanese car manufacturer had just gotten the okay to build a plant in Kentucky. They were getting a bunch of negative press from a lot of uninformed politicians and citizens who feared that the Japanese might have lost the big war but were winning the economic war against us, buying us out from under our own feet. The argument was insane. The US economy was ten times bigger than the Japanese economy and the plant was going to provide thousands of well-paying jobs with excellent benefits for the citizens of Kentucky. The car company executives were greatly concerned about their image. They did not want to open the plant and see a never-ending parade of protests right outside their doors.

I started to sketch Nancy, who was sitting in a beach chair reading, marking up another new Russian novel. I imagined the subject (Nancy) throwing her arms around her husband (subject #2) as he walked out of the car plant. They get into their new Japanese car and look in the back seat where a baby seat is attached. They smile at each other and start...

The phone rang. I picked it up on the second ring, just before Nancy picked up the pool phone that was right beside her. I didn't hear the usual click that you hear when someone on another extension hangs up.

I guess she didn't believe in privacy. She had no problem breaking into my house. Surely she was entitled to know with whom I was speaking. It was my precious Maggie sounding very apologetic. I reassured her that she had done nothing wrong and was quite entertaining.

"I didn't have any panties on when I woke up with all my other clothes on from last night. Did we have sex and I just don't remember?"

"No! You went to the bathroom and before you could pull your panties down you peed all over yourself. No big deal."

"I told you that?"

"Yes, you were very forthcoming last night."

"I was worried because I was ovulating yesterday and I didn't have any protection."

"Not to worry, sweetheart, nothing happened."

"If I didn't feel so messed up from last night I would come over there right now and fuck your brains out."

"That's very sweet of you, Maggie, but I think you really need more rest. And whatever you do, don't smoke anymore of that pot from yesterday. I think it might have been laced with something."

"I won't! I'm sure I'll feel better in a few hours. Maybe I can come over then and we can play doctor?"

"Wouldn't you rather stay at home and spend some quality time with the children?"

"No! That's why I have a full-time nanny. They like her better than me anyway."

"I seriously doubt that."

"Joe, I must have eaten an awful lot last night because I barfed up stuff I didn't recognize."

"You had a variety of wonderful dishes."

"Well, I'm happy it's all out of my system now. Otherwise I would have to spend ten hours at the gym tomorrow."

"Drink a lot of water, Maggie. I'll see you on Monday."

"I love you, Joe."

"I love you, too."

Maggie hung up, and, before Nancy could, I yelled into the phone. "Did you get all that, Nancy?"

"My God, you don't have to yell into the phone. How rude!"

I slammed the phone down as I saw her get up from the pool chair and walk toward the house. I looked at her as she sat down next to me.

"Seriously, Nancy, did no one ever teach you to respect people's privacy, especially when you're a guest?"

"I was curious."

"And that's supposed to make it right? What are you jealous of? Maggie? Is that it?"

She looked away from me and didn't say anything for a long moment.

"Yes, I am."

"Seriously, you're jealous of Maggie?"

She looked directly at me and replied, "Yes, Joe, I'm jealous of Maggie. I told you I don't lie."

"Everybody lies!"

"I don't, unless the truth is going to seriously hurt a good person. As much as I hate to admit it, I am jealous of that dimwit. I thought a guy like you would be smart enough not to fall for someone like her."

"She's my closest friend, maybe my only friend in this whole town."

"She's a friend with an awful lot of benefits attached to her. It's a good thing you two didn't have sex last night. I can only imagine what type of creature you would have produced."

I didn't give Nancy the satisfaction of an answer. Maggie and I would have had beautiful children together, sons or daughters who looked like Maggie. Her two children, though terribly misbehaved, were adorable.

I suddenly noticed a chain with the Star of David attached hanging from Nancy's neck. "What's with the Star of David? Looking for divine intervention to help you with your lack of social skills?"

"Excuse me," she replied angrily. "You don't see me making fun of the crucifix around your neck."

"That's because I always wear it. It was a gift from my mother. This is the first time I've seen you wearing that chain."

"How do you know it wasn't in the shop getting fixed?"

"Because you don't have any money."

"True enough."

"Believe me, I'm overjoyed to know that you believe in something bigger than yourself."

"Very funny. I'm wearing it as a sort of experiment. A cause-and-effect type of thing."

"Of course you are. How foolish of me to think you were wearing it for any other reason."

"Did you enjoy watching me swim?"

"What type of question is that?"

"A simple yes or no is all that's required. I usually wear a one-piece bathing suit when I swim, but I figured you would be more interested if you thought at any moment the top would come off and you would get to see my boobs."

"I've already seen your boobs. Do I look like a teenager?"

"No, but I'm fairly sure that's exactly what you were hoping for. Once covered, they become a whole new fascination."

"Wow! You really do think of yourself as a goddess."

"No, I don't — but you do." She got up from the chair and started walking away, untying her bikini top and flinging it over her head. It landed at my feet. "I'm going to take a shower. Please don't interrupt. I like my privacy and I am in no mood to fuck anyone's brains out."

I was tempted to leave the house and go straight to Maggie's. But then I thought better of it ... her children, their mother hungover, and that nanny with the bad attitude. That situation was actually worse than having to deal with Nancy the stuck-up goddess.

I went back to my sketches but discarded that idea, then went into the kitchen and grabbed a bottle of chardonnay.

Nancy reappeared, her hair wet from the shower, wearing one of my dress shirts and nothing else that I could see. She was combing her hair, slowly, teasing like a model in one of my commercials. I was convinced at that moment that she was either trying to drive me mad or make me die of a heart attack while drooling over her like a pathetic fool.

"Do you have any clothes of your own?" I asked. She laughed.

"A little early to be drinking?"

"Not when you're around."

She sat down on the couch beside me, took the glass out of my hand, and took a large sip. "Why don't you get yourself a glass?"

"It's more romantic this way." She handed me back the glass and laid her head in my lap. "The only thing missing are some grapes for you to feed me."

"Very biblical, like your Star of David."

"The Star of David didn't come into existence until the seventeenth century. It isn't even mentioned in the Bible."

"I didn't know that."

"I'm surprised, considering how many Jewish customers your firm must have as clients."

"I doubt any of my Jewish clients would know that."

"Oh, I forgot … your clients are mainly the unethical type. The only religion they know is peddling lies and accumulating large profits."

She lifted her head, took the glass out of my hand, and had another big sip.

"You don't know anything about my clients and business associates."

"You'd be surprised at what I know." She laid her head back down and looked up at me with those big blue eyes. "No need to get defensive. Do you think your parents would be happy with your wealth and success?"

"I don't see why not. Surprised, but happy."

"Surprised? Why's that? You don't think they expected much from you?"

"Before I went to college, I was a classic underachiever."

"It's a real shame they didn't get to live longer and see what their only child has accomplished. I think they would be very proud."

"Are you being sarcastic?"

"Absolutely not. I might dislike the type of work you do, but I respect you as a person and your achievements. I wouldn't be here right now if I didn't see the overwhelming goodness in you and the many wonderful qualities you possess."

"Thanks, Nancy!" That was a refreshing and unexpected compliment. I braced myself for the follow-up.

"Do you plan on using my image you were sketching in a campaign?"

"Not without your consent. And you'll get paid."

"What are you selling?"

"A car."

"Just a car or a company that manufactures cars?"

"A company. They're getting a lot of bad press about a plant they want to build down south."

"A foreign company. I read about it. No, I don't want you to use my image."

"Okay. I'll use Maggie instead."

"Good, why don't you do that? Apparently, your precious little assistant has no problem selling herself."

"She understands the importance of money and I don't remember her ever borrowing any from me."

"I'm keeping track of the money I've borrowed."

"I know! I imagine you're really good at math."

"I'm exceptional. After we get married, can I turn one of those empty rooms at the back of the house into a study for myself?"

"Wow! That's a leap forward."

"Why? We're a perfect match."

She lifted her head up and took the glass again, her wet hair leaving a spot on my pants. "You don't think so?" she asked in an unbelieving tone, as if questioning her statement and deduction was an insult.

"Do you remember some of the things you've said to me? The criticisms that sting like an Ali punch?"

"Surely you're smart enough to know that critiques are meant to be constructive and enlightening."

"You're joking," I replied, and she stared at me like I was an experiment in stupidity.

"No, I'm not joking! Frankly, I'm shocked you don't see our similarities."

"I've known you for four days, Nancy. Granted, an eventful four days, but four days all the same."

"Most guys ask me to marry them after a few hours."

"That's because they haven't been stung as many times as I have."

"Wow! You're even less of a man than I thought."

"There you go again. Do you even listen to the things that come out of your mouth?"

She stood up and bent over to grab the bottle of wine, and in so doing put her bare ass right up against my face. Never did such a lovely butt deserve a really good spanking. She quickly turned and in one motion gave me a full-frontal view of her lower anatomy.

"It was a suggestion, a simple hint that I was open to the idea of marrying you, but now it's more obvious than ever that your darling Maggie has the inside track on that."

"Maggie's been married and divorced twice. She has two children. I imagine if I wanted to, I could have been her first or second husband. It's silly to think that I'm aiming to be her third, especially with those obnoxious kids I'd inherit."

She looked down at me as she fiddled with the Star of David around her neck. "Interesting how my little experiment is yielding results even quicker than I could have predicted."

"What is that supposed to mean?" She filled the wine glass again and started walking back toward the pool area.

"How about leaving me my glass?"

"How about you get your sorry ass off the couch and get yourself another glass?"

I got my sorry ass off the couch, walked into the kitchen, and got myself another glass. I walked back into the living room and there she was, standing by the couch.

"What's wrong?" I asked. She looked quite confused and devoid of her usual self-confidence.

"Nothing!"

"I thought you never lie."

"I don't. I'm just a little tired and didn't want to fall asleep in the sun."

She sat down on the couch and I sat down beside her. I filled my glass with wine and asked, "Where's your glass?"

"I left it outside." She took my glass, had a sip, and put the glass on the table. She placed her head against my chest and hugged me. "I slept so well like this last night." She fell asleep quickly as I ran my hand through her hair. There are moments, mere seconds of profound awareness, in which our lives are redefined and the disguises our friends and loved ones wear are unmasked. And the knowledge we attain during these brief flashes of discovery and revelation defines the trustworthiness and honesty that we seek in ourselves and cherish in others.

Nancy's grip around my waist was tight. She trusted me in a way I don't think she ever trusted another person, and unmasked her vulnerabilities for the one person she knew would understand.

She slept for a couple of hours and announced upon waking that she was starving. We decided to eat lunch at a French restaurant in Studio City. She put on a pair of my underwear and flip-flops and was about to walk out the door when I grabbed her by the arm and told her there was no way we were going out in public with her barely dressed. She walked back into my bedroom and took out a pair of my pants from my closet. She pinned the pants up and attached a pair of suspenders to keep the pants from falling.

"How do I look?"

"Like a beautiful hobo dressed in very expensive clothes, but at least you won't be starting any riots dressed like that."

Chapter Eight

The maître d' sat us toward the back of the restaurant. The poor fellow couldn't help but stare at Nancy's breasts, which were quite visible through the gaps in the shirt she wore.

She rudely asked, "Have you never seen a woman's breasts before?"

He blushed and I quickly ordered an expensive bottle of red wine. Last night's adventure with Maggie had put me on full alert. I wasn't about to repeat anything remotely similar to that nightmare. The maître d' walked away as I reached over and buttoned Nancy's shirt. "What? You don't like the view?"

"Don't be silly, I love the view." I lifted her head up and looked directly into her face. "It's the most magnificent view I've ever seen."

"Thank you, Joe. I promise not to tell if you promise to stop fucking Maggie."

I wasn't quite sure how to respond to her remark so I didn't. The headwaiter came over and opened the bottle of wine. I had Nancy taste the wine and like a real professional she swirled it around in her glass, smelled the bouquet, and took a small taste. She paused as she looked at me with her mirthful blue eyes. "Lovely." The waiter filled our glasses halfway and left us to look at the menus.

"So are you enjoying Dostoevsky's *Crime and Punishment*?"

"It was marvelous. I finished it this morning after I left your place."

"You finished that nearly 600-page book in a day?"

"I process words very quickly. The main character, Rodin Raskolnikov, reminded me of you."

"No, he didn't. I don't even know where you come off making such a statement." I was angry. She was comparing me to a student who kills a pawnbroker because he thinks the world would be better off without such an evil person.

"Maybe if you read my notes you would better understand the similarities."

"I don't need to read your stupid notes to know that you're totally off the mark."

"Why so defensive, Joe?"

"I'm not being defensive. Just don't insult my intelligence by telling me that a character who commits murder reminds you of me."

"The murder was a symbolic stimulus to push the story forward. It was more about the undercover exploration of the Russian psyche and how the environment and culture affect the Russian people."

"Great! Why don't you go ahead and write a thesis on the book? Just don't bother giving me a copy."

"I thought you would appreciate an intelligent conversation about one of the greatest novels ever written."

"Yes, an intelligent conversation, not a critique of me and the work I do."

"Sorry you feel that way." She half-apologetically looked at me over the menu.

"I must ask, do you drive?"

"I have a driver's license, but no car. I crashed my car into a fire hydrant, which was the end of both the car and the hydrant. I just thank God no one got hurt."

"How did you accomplish that feat? Jotting down a few notes instead of paying attention to the road?"

"Glanced down at a book I was reading and got caught up in the narrative. It was late at night. I still have to pay for the hydrant; I destroyed city property."

"Does that make you feel stupid, or were you able to rationalize it and blame it all on the stationary object that got in your way?"

"I don't need to rationalize. It was plainly my fault."

"Wow! That must have been really hard for you to admit — taking responsibility for an unwise act."

"No, you're wrong. Admitting I'm jealous of that dimwit Maggie is hard, not crashing into a fire hydrant."

"She's really under your skin. You call her a dimwit but from where I'm standing you're the loser. And by the way, she doesn't think very highly of you either."

"Does it make you feel powerful that two women are vying for your attention?"

"No, because there aren't two women vying for my attention. That competition is taking place solely in your deductive-hallucinogenic mind."

Nancy picked up a piece of a baguette and lightly buttered it. She bit off tiny pieces and chewed slowly, watching me like a superior being studying a less-evolved creature.

"What? A little tongue-tied?"

"Is that what you think, Joe? That a few insults thrown my way could so easily faze me?"

"No, I'm not that stupid. You only show your vulnerabilities when you have the security of a little shell to crawl into."

"I don't even know what that's supposed to mean."

"Sure you do, Nancy. A superior creature like you can figure out anything. Just apply a little deductive reasoning to the riddle."

"Why are you behaving like an asshole?"

I picked up my glass of wine and took a sip. "You're right, the wine is lovely, and if I am behaving like an asshole, it's in response to your elitist attitude and unfounded comments."

"I am going to order the boeuf bourguignon."

"Funny, an elitist ordering a stew."

"I'm not going to argue with you, Joe." She continued eating tiny pieces of the bread, sipping her wine, and staring at me with untold curiosity.

"Is there something you see in my face that I've missed all these years of looking into mirrors?"

"No. You just have a nice face and despite your irascible attitude at the moment, I know you are nothing like that."

I also ordered the boeuf bourguignon and another bottle of wine.

The meal was delicious, and after three bottles of wine all my bravado had dissipated. All I could think about was burying my head between Nancy's breasts. I was quite sure she knew exactly what I was contemplating and as if to send the point smashing home, she unbuttoned the top button on her shirt. She ordered crème brulée for dessert then slowly and deliberately picked at it.

"You know, if you had been a little nicer earlier, I had planned a wonderful dessert when we got home."

"Has anyone ever told you you're a real bitch?"

"Not to my face, but I'm sure plenty of people have said it behind my back."

I ordered a double espresso and a Sandeman Founder's Reserve port.

"You know, Joe, caffeine won't sober you up. It might make you a little more alert, but that's it."

"Thanks for that useful piece of information."

I felt her foot working its way up my leg under the table and coming to an abrupt stop at my crotch.

"I see you're thinking about ordering something off the menu."

"Nothing that concerns you."

"You know, it's about five hours since you spoke to Maggie. I'm sure she's ready and willing to go by now. She did say in a few hours?"

"She's definitely a better option than you."

Nancy moved forward just enough to give me a clear view of her breasts.

"Do you really mean that, Joe? Or are you just talking trash?"

The waiter placed the espresso and port down. "You might want to bring her the same," I said to the waiter.

"Decaffeinated, please, and a double port. I'm about as alert as I need to be right now."

"Why not call Maggie? I'm all in for a threesome," Nancy offered.

"It would be a shame to even mention such a thing to Maggie. Besides, I would feel guilty about spending all my time with Maggie and having you feel unwanted."

"Oh, that's thoughtful, Joe, but don't you worry. I'm fairly sure your precious Maggie is more than capable of satisfying me in ways you couldn't imagine. In many ways, once Maggie and I get started on each other you'd probably be nothing more than an afterthought."

"You really are one pompous, self-serving little minx. What college did you graduate from, USC?"

"No, MIT. Massachusetts Institute of Technology."

"I don't believe you."

"I told you, I don't lie." Nancy reached into her purse and pulled out a student ID card from MIT with her picture on it. She handed it to me and I looked at it carefully. "When did you graduate?"

"Five years ago, at the tender age of nineteen. To be fair, I started a year early, at seventeen."

"You graduated one of the most prestigious universities in the country in two years?"

"Two and a half. I process information very quickly." She reached back into her purse and took out another student ID from Stanford University. "I did my post-graduate studies at Stanford." I looked at the Stanford ID, shook my head, and handed both cards back to her.

"Why are you doing makeup? You could be teaching and doing research at any university or laboratory in the world. You could be working for the government and making a fortune."

"I'm exactly where I want to be."

"Making talentless shitheads look pretty."

"Working with chemicals."

The waiter brought Nancy's drinks as I tried to understand this beautiful, apparently brilliant, befuddling woman in front of me. She had suddenly turned into a giant brain with big blue eyes and voluptuous breasts. I thought about reaching over and touching her, but I instead asked for the check. I paid, had the waiter call us a cab, and back to my house we went. I was tired and couldn't quite figure out how I'd gotten so drunk. Nancy, who drank just as much, seemed perfectly fine, or as normal as one could expect from a lunatic. I started to suspect that she had drugged me and was waiting for me to pass out so she could experiment on my far less-superior brain.

I told her I was going to the bathroom but instead went into my bedroom and locked the door, as if that would keep her out. I thought about putting a chair up against the lock of the door, but before I could do that, I fell down flat on my bed and fell asleep.

I woke up about six hours later and the door to my room was open. The sound of Duke Ellington came from the living room and all my clothes were still on. My brain felt fried but I was pretty sure that was from the booze. I stumbled into the living room and looked at Nancy's bare ass. She was lying on the couch, dressed in one of my Armani sport coats, reading Dostoevsky's *Brothers Karamazov* — a brief, 850-page masterpiece from the Russian genius. I gently touched her bare ass and she slowly turned around as though she'd been expecting me.

"Feeling better, sleepyhead?"

"Not really." I sat down on the couch. She sat up and put my head in her lap. She ran her hand through my hair, and I couldn't find the courage to ask her what happened. Instead I asked, "How do you like the book?"

"Great, but not as brilliant as *Crime and Punishment*. He could have easily cut a hundred pages. The part about the priest's decaying body was chilling. What do you think it meant?"

"I think it was a reminder that human beings, regardless of how brilliant, compassionate, and loving they are, are still not God. Like all people, our bodies will decay after death. Despite all the accolades and reverence people might have for the deceased, we aren't coming back to this life and we rule over nothing here."

"That's how I analyzed it, too. Thank you for introducing me to such a great writer."

She continued to run her hands through my hair and even though my head ached terribly, it felt soothing.

"Did your mommy have thick and beautiful hair like you?"

"Yes, and my father, too."

"They must have been a very attractive couple to produce such a handsome son."

"I think so."

"And did they love each other?"

"They adored each other. Why would you ask such a question?"

"Just curious, that's all. It's too bad they didn't have more children."

"I'm sure they wanted to but couldn't."

"You would have made a wonderful big brother. You protect the people you love, don't you, Joe?"

I rearranged my head on her lap and looked up at her. Her overwhelming beauty never failed to amaze me, and her level of concentration was equally breathtaking. It was as though she had some superpower that allowed her to see right through to the atoms and molecules that make up our existence. She lowered her gaze and looked down into my eyes. I couldn't read her.

"What are you thinking about, Nancy?"

"It's not important."

"It is to me." She laughed and shrugged off the question. "Are you going to be here when I wake up?" I asked.

"Probably not."

"But you'll be back in the morning?"

"Probably not. I have a lot of work to get done."

"You can do it here. I won't disturb you."

"Is this your way of saying you're going to miss me?"

"Yes."

Nancy looked up as she continued to run her hands through my hair. I closed my eyes to the sound of her soft breathing, which seemed to drown out all other noises. When I woke up hours later, she was gone.

She didn't come back or call that day. I couldn't call her because I didn't have her home phone number. I was tempted to call the cab company and ask where they dropped her off, but decided against it. I walked to the French restaurant and picked up my car.

The rest of the day I relaxed and polished the presentation I was going to give to the Japanese auto executives the next day.

Chapter Nine

Maggie was already at her desk when I got to work. She had this unnatural glow about her and her eyes were glassy and glazed over. I didn't smell anything to make me suspect she'd been smoking marijuana, but she was wearing this unusual perfume that led me to her like a teenage boy visiting a French brothel.

I shook the urge off. It wasn't easy, but a flashback to her face in a bowl of lasagna helped alleviate it.

"Jack wants his book back," she said to me in the most condescending tone. "You know, the album with all the hookers."

"How do you know about that?"

"The janitor told me. I never would've suspected you were into that."

"I'm not."

"Of course not," she said unconvincingly as I handed her the portfolio with the drawings and slogans we were going to use during the presentation. She put it aside as though it was of no importance.

"Are you okay?"

"I'm wonderful." She attempted a weak smile.

"Are you high?" I asked as she turned her back to me.

"Just a little taken aback by the book."

I turned her chair around to face me and held on to its arms. "The book is none of your concern, and I find it highly insulting that you would think I would be sharing women with Jack."

"Whatever…"

"Seriously, Maggie, you're calling me a liar?"

"It's what we do around here. Isn't that what you always say?"

"But not between us. We've always been truthful with each other."

"I guess…"

She tried to turn the chair around again, but I held on tight. "What the hell is going on with you lately? Are you wearing a new perfume?"

"Do you like it?"

"What's not to like? What are you trying to do, start your own harem?"

"Only you."

"You can do better than me." I let go of her chair and stepped back.

"Why don't you let me decide what's best for me?" She winked. Why was Maggie acting like this now when we'd agreed we didn't want to go down that road together? Other than a few crazy times early on, we'd kept it professional. That's probably the only reason we were able to remain such good friends and work together so well. It's the reason Jack selected his rotating partners from a photo album of strangers. Sex complicates otherwise healthy relationships.

I decided to shift the focus to work. "Would you please look at the portfolio? The presentation is at two this afternoon."

"I know, Joe. I have it written down. We have plenty of time."

I walked into my office and grabbed Jack's book. I wasn't sure what was going on with Maggie, but whatever it was, it was working. It was like she had hooked me and was getting ready to reel me in. All of her glances and gestures were suggestive. It had been a long time since we'd been intimate. I tried to ignore this new energy she was giving off, but it was powerful. And that perfume … I tried to shake the feeling, but it took effort.

I averted my eyes when walking past her on my way to Jack's office. She didn't make it easy. "What a disgusting pig our fearless leader is," she commented. Quickly glancing at her, I continued on my mission.

I knocked on Jack's door but there was no answer. I could hear movement in the office, so I turned the knob but the door was locked. A second later, Jack opened the door slightly and stuck his head out.

"Joe, what is it?" he asked in a hushed voice. I handed him the book.

"The Japanese executives are here for a presentation at two o'clock."

"You have it under control?"

"Yeah!"

"Great! I'll provide the entertainment."

He closed the door and from inside the office I could hear a female Russian voice say, "Come here my little Любовник." From the sexy tone of her voice, I didn't need a translator to tell me what was going on inside.

I walked toward my office and stopped at Maggie's desk. She was looking over the portfolio. "What do you think?" I asked. She looked up at me and didn't say a word. After a few uncomfortable moments of silence, I walked into my office. She followed me, locked the door, and flung the portfolio off to the side. "I guess you didn't like it," I said.

Maggie closed all the blinds on the office windows. "Shut up, Joe, and sit down." This was a demand, as she literally forced me into my desk chair. Before I could say anything she had slipped all her clothes off, except for her bra and panties, and sat on my lap. It was futile for me even to try to resist, especially since my anatomy was already saying *Yes.*

"You know this could get us fired, right? Against company policy."

She laughed as she undid my belt and opened my pants.

"Protection?" I asked.

"Don't be silly, I've been planning this all weekend." She took total control, and I submitted without any further struggle.

After it was over, I lay on the floor with my head against the couch. I struggled to get my underwear on as Maggie lay naked on the sofa above me.

"You've gone to school since the last time we had sex."

"You complaining?"

"No, a few of those positions I never knew existed."

"You know, Joe, I feel so relaxed right now. It would be a great idea if employees were allowed to fuck at work. Just think how much more relaxed and content the staff would be."

"Maybe you should bring that up at the next staff meeting."

She laughed as she sat up and wrapped her long legs around my neck. "You didn't think we were finished?"

Once again, my other brain was doing the speaking for me. Maggie lowered her head and started kissing me.

A half hour later, I was back in the same position on the floor with my head against the couch. I was physically exhausted. Maggie lay resting on the couch, still naked. Apparently, sex really did relax her. When I told her we needed to get dressed before people got suspicious, she just laughed. I struggled to get my clothes back on while Maggie didn't move.

"I'm serious, Maggie, you need to get dressed."

"The only thing I need to do is take a nap. Throw your jacket over me, please. I'm a little chilly."

I didn't have the energy to argue. I just did what she asked. Before I had time to turn around, she was already asleep.

I sat at my desk and picked up the portfolio but couldn't concentrate. I felt like a prisoner in my own office. The blinds were shut, the door locked, and every employee on the floor knew damn well what was going on in here. Maggie had made sure of that. Despite my continual warnings and pleading for her to be quiet, she screamed so loud that they could probably hear her down in the lobby.

If I had asked myself just a few days ago which one was crazier, Nancy or Maggie, the answer would have been simple: Nancy, by a long shot. But Maggie was gaining ground quickly, and her latest performance put her in the lead.

The phone rang, and since my lovely assistant was in no position to pick it up, I did the honors. Who else but Nancy was on the other end?

"Hello, Joe. I thought your beautiful assistant screened all your calls. Where might she be? Cleaning up after the two of you fucked all morning?"

"I don't have time for this nonsense, Nancy. I have a very important presentation to give just after lunch and I'm still not totally prepared."

"Well, maybe if you didn't waste so much time screwing your precious little Maggie, you wouldn't be so behind."

"What is it that you want, Nancy?"

"No need to be rude. I just want to know if you can drive me to the airport in the morning. My flight is at ten but you can pick me up at six. I wouldn't want you to be late to work and miss out on any activities you might have planned."

I closed my eyes and thought to myself, *Why am I taking this bullshit? Why is she such a psychotic bitch? Why do I get caught up with women who twist my world around? Why?*

"How about I just give you money for a cab?"

"No! I really want to see you without the scent of that dimwit on you. Please, just drive me. Please."

"Okay," I said like a pussy-whipped little boy. She didn't want to come over after work because as she said, she "didn't want to smell the stench of that bitch." It was too ironic for me to argue. I agreed to pick her up outside her apartment the following morning. After hanging up, there was no doubt in my mind that Nancy was once again out in front in the crazy department.

It was time to go meet the Japanese delegation. The lobby receptionist called and told me they had just arrived. The conference room was set up with a screen and a slideshow presentation. Japanese executives liked to look at pictures and moving images — possibly because many of them didn't speak or understand English, or maybe they pretended not to. I made a few adjustments to the portfolio, but I would only use it if I felt I had lost their interest. Everything I needed was already set up in the conference room.

I didn't bother waking Sleeping Beauty. She was so out of it that for the first time in all our years working together, I believed she might do some serious damage and possibly cost us a lucrative contract. Maggie was usually a key asset, especially when the executives we were trying to impress were all men, and usually execs from Japanese companies were all men. I didn't know what the hell she was on, but I couldn't take a chance even after she had been asleep for four hours. I left her in my office.

I greeted the delegation in the lobby. There were eight executives, an American consultant, and a translator. They were impeccably dressed, polite, and keenly aware of their surroundings.

The presentation seemed to be going well, even though with Japanese businessmen it was hard to tell. They seemed to gravitate to the idea of presenting their company, not as an outside force, but as an opportunity for real growth and well-paying jobs for the people of Kentucky. I stressed the idea of assimilation and for the company to embrace the concept of "family values" that were so important to the people of this state. I emphasized that the majority of Kentucky is Christian, and the people take their religion very seriously. More than half of our planned advertising included subtle, positive references to the powerful religious influences throughout the state.

The executives listened carefully to the translator and occasionally bowed their heads in agreement. Suddenly, I turned my attention to the door and saw Maggie walking straight toward me. She was dressed in my sport coat and her high heels and nothing else. Her breasts were barely covered, and as she threw her arms around me and kissed me on the mouth, her bare ass was visible to everyone.

She turned toward the executives and said, "We're in love." They all stood up and started to applaud enthusiastically. As she bowed, she again revealed her bare ass to the people who might have missed it the first time. They continued to clap even after she left; the translator turned to me and said, "I think you won them over."

I continued the presentation, but after Maggie's performance they didn't seem very interested. They asked the translator her name, and then they started chanting, "Maggie! Maggie! Maggie!"

If this wasn't enough to drive me crazy, Jack walked into the room and started shaking everyone's hand as though he knew them all. Instantly, all the executives started speaking English and warmly embracing Jack as though they had known each other for years.

Jack took me by the shoulders and said to the crowd, "The best! The very best!" They once again started to clap and Jack whispered to me, "Meet us downstairs in the dining area. Lobster and Russian hookers are being served." They followed Jack out of the conference room as I stood there in a state of amazement.

I walked back to my office ready to tear into Maggie, but when I opened the door and found her eating a chocolate cupcake like an eight-year-old, I didn't have the heart. All I came up with was a pathetic, "Where did you get the cupcake?"

"The boys in the lobby." She pointed to a box of cupcakes on the desk. "Have one, they're delicious."

I picked up a cupcake and sat down next to her on the couch. "So, how did it go?"

"Wonderful! They're in love with you."

"Happy I could help."

The cupcake was delicious, but my senses were once again overtaken by the smell of Maggie's perfume, the same scent that had started the day's bizarre chain of events. Within seconds, Maggie and I were at it again. I didn't even bother to muffle her insanely loud moans and groans. I was undeniably a pig, no different from Jack. Maybe I was worse … taking advantage of a deranged woman. Something in that perfume drove me crazy. It was intoxicating.

After we finished, Maggie lay with her head down on my naked lap and started to cry. "I'm nothing more than a despicable whore; a dirty, low-life whore."

"Why would you say such a thing? That's crazy talk."

"Why? Because I lied to you, Joe. I'm not using any protection; I'm not on any birth control. We just fucked all day and I let you come inside me over and over again."

"Why on earth would you do such a thing? This doesn't make any sense, Maggie. It isn't like you. None of this."

"I'm just a dirty, despicable, low-life whore…" She started crying again.

I ordered Maggie to get dressed in her own clothes and stay in the office. I took her car keys out of her purse and went downstairs to the dining area, where Jack was entertaining the Japanese executives with an assortment of Russian hookers, lobster, champagne, and Budweiser beer.

The second I entered the dining area, the executives started chanting, "Maggie! Maggie! Maggie!" I made up a sad excuse that she wasn't feeling well and had to go home.

When I left the dining area, I was fully confident that Jack had the situation under control. Suddenly, I felt pangs of guilt. Maggie really wasn't feeling well. She was clearly not herself. I had sensed that she was high as a kite but nevertheless had sex with her several times that day. She was an adult and might have lied, but I was just as responsible as she was. Whatever consequences might follow, I would share owning it and help her deal with it.

When I got back to my office I almost didn't recognize Maggie fully dressed. She was sitting at my desk, looking into a mirror and fixing her hair. I lifted her up and embraced her tightly. Today had been crazy and out of character for both of us. I cared about her and would never abandon her.

Maggie sat in the passenger seat, nodding off. If I didn't know better I would have thought she was on heroin — was that possible? I tried to keep my eyes on the road as I drove along Sunset Boulevard toward Maggie's home in Brentwood. The twists and turns on the Boulevard could be quite tricky and dangerous, and even though I had been on this road just a few days ago, I still felt uncomfortable driving it, especially at night.

We stopped at a red light just before UCLA. I looked at Maggie, who was reaching between her legs with her fingers and then rubbing her fingers against her lips. "What are you doing?"

"I'm leaking."

"Leaking what?"

"What do you think, Joe?"

"Stop that, Maggie! That's absolutely disgusting!"

"Maybe you should have thought about that before we had sex."

She reached deep inside her vagina as though searching for some foreign object and then suddenly pulled out a flexible rubber cup. She looked at it in confusion then remarked, "I guess you're off the hook."

"What are you talking about?"

"It's a diaphragm. Surely you've fucked enough women to know what a diaphragm is. I don't remember putting it in, but you're off the hook. We both are." She slapped the diaphragm onto my crotch. "Why don't you keep it as a trophy? A reminder of your conquest over me."

I picked the object off my lap and flung it out the window. Then I reached for a box of tissues in the back seat to dry off my wet crotch, cleaning the area as well as I could under the circumstances. Handing the box to Maggie, I said, "Please, clean yourself. Please."

She totally ignored me, staring ahead like a zombie. The light changed and we drove the rest of the way to her house without a word. For the second time in four days, I had to carry her into her house and put her in bed.

As I turned out of Maggie's driveway and back onto Sunset, I realized that the players had switched places yet again. Earlier today I could not imagine any woman more unstable or crazy than Nancy. But after tonight and that episode in the car earlier, I wasn't at all sure anymore.

They were running neck and neck, and, by having sex with both of them, I was only adding fuel to an already out-of-control, raging fire. Since having her children, Maggie had regularly shown me pictures of them. She might have married her two husbands for their money, but she loved and adored her children and was exceptionally overprotective of them. As for her ex-husbands, they knew exactly what they were getting into when marrying Maggie, so I had no sympathy for them. They wanted a stunning young wife to show off to their Hollywood buddies, and dishing out a few million dollars in alimony and a house in Brentwood after they were tired of her was worth it. After all, you're nothing in Hollywood unless you have a few ex-wives to bitch about.

The thing that troubled me was that Maggie had suddenly seemed to lose interest in her kids. It was like they didn't exist and from what I could see and hear, the nanny had taken full responsibility for feeding, clothing, bathing, and taking them to and from preschool. Maggie wasn't even tucking the kids in at night, and it wasn't like she didn't have the time.

It was all very troublesome, and I couldn't wait to get home and have a few cold beers, but first I decided to stop at a bookstore in Studio City. Bookstar was originally an old movie theater, and it had recently been turned into a large, beautiful bookstore with an amazing selection of new and old books. Against my better judgment, I bought every book they had by any famous Russian authors, from Dostoevsky and Tolstoy to Turgenev. I even picked up Joseph Conrad's masterpiece *Under Western Eyes*, which dealt with a Russian revolutionary turned traitor, who was eventually exiled to England instead of being shot in exchange for information he gave the government on a fellow revolutionary. The fellow revolutionary was naturally killed, but in a strange twist of fate, he turned out to be the brother of the girl the traitor falls in love with while in England. If this all sounds a little confusing, well, that's because it is. Everything concerning Russia and its people is confusing — well, except for the Russian whores Jack had hired to entertain the Japanese executives.

The books were for Nancy. I figured they'd be a nice gift she could take on her trip. I knew it was already an explosive situation, but she deserved a chance to again take a healthy lead over the ever-encroaching Maggie.

I felt dirty, but the desire for a beer was more overwhelming than the need for a shower. The first five went down so well that I took my sixth beer into the shower with me. The idea that soap and water might wash away the day was absurd, but the beer could at least help me forget.

The phone rang just as I was drying off. Nancy reminded me to pick her up tomorrow morning at six. She was curt, obviously wondering if an intellectually challenged creature like myself might forget if she didn't remind me.

After my short conversation with Nancy, I called my friend George. He was a limousine driver for the company, taking clients to and from the airport when they were in town. I asked if George could pick me up at a quarter to six and drive me to the airport. He said no problem. I always tipped him handsomely and we understood each other perfectly.

I knew I would be in no condition in the morning to listen to Nancy and drive at the same time. I walked over to the stereo and put on a Sinatra album as I cracked open another beer.

Chapter Ten

I woke up about five-fifteen in the morning, feeling a little dazed and confused from the previous night's drinking. I took another shower, and George arrived at exactly a quarter to six. We drove less than a mile to pick up Nancy. She was standing, looking stunning, outside her building with a small suitcase beside her. George exclaimed, "Wow!"

"Yes, wow says it all," I replied as George pulled up next to Nancy. I got out of the car and helped Nancy with her suitcase. "You didn't have to rent a limo," she remarked as we both got into the car.

"I didn't. This is a company limo and George works for us."

"Hello, George," Nancy said politely as she reached over and shook his hand. "So you're in the business of lying, too."

George shook his head as I replied, "Don't mind her, George. The only thing more alarming than her astonishing beauty is the nonsense that comes out of her uncensored mouth."

Nancy slapped my arm. "That's mean. Sorry if I offended you, George."

"No problem." George drove on and Nancy cuddled up next to me.

"So, where are you going?" I asked.

"New Mexico."

"Why New Mexico?"

"I was invited to a convention on physics."

"The type of convention someone like me would never be invited to?"

"If you say so."

"How long will you be gone?"

"Four days. I come back Friday night. If you're not doing anything, you could pick me up. I arrive at eight o'clock."

She looked at me with her big blue eyes and I was transfixed. I could feel my heart racing.

"I'm pretty certain I can manage that," I replied.

"Great!"

I was waiting for her to bring up "that despicable little whore Maggie" but she never mentioned her. I figured that was a calculated move on her part. As we got close to the airport I asked, "So where are you staying in New Mexico?"

"I don't know. You know me, I'll figure something out." I took that to mean she would be screwing some celebrated physicist and staying in his hotel room for the next four days. I took out my wallet and handed her one of my credit cards.

"I want you to get a nice hotel room. If they give you a problem, simply tell them you're my wife and have them call me."

"Is this your way of proposing?"

"If that's the way you want to see it, that's fine. Just promise me, no guests."

"I promise, if you promise me the same thing. No sleepovers at Rancho José."

"I promise."

"Great! I'll behave like a nun and you behave like a monk, and when I get back we can screw like two virgin honeymooners," she whispered into my ear.

"How much money do you have on you, Nancy?"

"Thirty dollars."

I shook my head and fought back the urge to chastise her. Once again I reached into my wallet and handed her $300.

"I'm never going to be able to pay you back."

"Have I ever implied that I expected you to pay me back?"

"No."

I reached over and handed her the shopping bag filled with half the books I bought the night before.

"A little going-away gift. The rest of the books I bought you are at the house. Now that you're going to behave like a nun, you should have plenty of time to read and take notes while not attending lectures."

She looked in the bag and her eyes seemed to grow even larger. You would have thought I had given her the biggest diamond ring the world had ever seen. She threw her arms around me and kissed me passionately.

"I love you so much … so much, so much!"

George parked next to the American terminal and I grabbed Nancy's luggage as she reached into her purse and tried to hand George a hundred-dollar tip. He refused as I slapped her hand. "What in God's creation is wrong with you?"

She grabbed her bag of books and stepped out of the limo. "I just wanted him to know how much I appreciate him driving me here."

"He knows, Nancy. Believe me, he knows."

I carried her luggage into the terminal and walked her to the security checkpoint. "Are you going to miss me?" She asked the question in almost a pleading way.

"Of course I'm going to miss you."

I reached over, took her head into my hands, and kissed her forehead. "Have a good time and don't forget to behave." We kissed passionately and I started walking away. When I looked back one last time, she was still standing in the same place and smiled at me.

As I walked back toward the limo, I felt this bizarre and uncomfortable feeling come over me. The only other time I could recall such a feeling was when I said goodbye to my parents and went off to college. I guess one could call it separation anxiety, even though I had only known Nancy for a short time and would be seeing her again in a few days. Or maybe it was fear that I might never see her again.

I opened the door to the limo and jumped in. I lay my head back on the seat and simply looked up as I waited for George to pull away.

"It must have been a difficult choice between Maggie and Nancy," George remarked.

"Why would you say that?"

George didn't answer as he deftly pulled away from the curb and into traffic.

"Let me guess, Maggie told you something like we were engaged?"

"Something like that. She said the only thing holding you back from announcing your intentions was that you were still deciding on what size ring to get her."

I looked straight ahead and asked, "Have you noticed anything strange about Maggie lately?"

Once again he didn't answer, and I continued, "I care about Maggie, and I've had to drive her home twice just this week because she was so out of it. Her behavior has been unpredictable and outrageous. I'm really starting to worry."

"She started seeing this guy a couple of months back. He drove a fancy car, dressed in expensive suits, and wined and dined her like he was some big-shot billionaire. Then he was gone. In short, he played her."

"Maggie doesn't get played. She's the one who does the playing."

"Well, this guy got her hooked on that new drug that's all over the streets — a combination of heroin, cocaine, and amphetamine. It comes in pill form and it's highly addictive after using it just a few times. From what I heard, he stole all of Maggie's savings in just a few months then had her borrow a ton of money using her house as collateral."

"I didn't know anything about this."

"She was too ashamed to tell you. She desperately needs help, Joe. I don't like to get involved. I hear lots of stuff from the driver's seat. Mostly I keep my mouth shut and mind my business. But Maggie is a sweet girl and has two kids. I figure if anyone can help her, it's you."

George dropped me off at my house. I walked inside, grabbed my car keys, and immediately drove to the office. It was still early and I didn't expect anyone to be there, but just as I got off the elevator I bumped into Jack, the last person I expected to find. Then again, there was a good chance he never left the building last night. He immediately put his arm around my shoulder and led me into his office. The man reeked of cigar smoke, booze, and need I say, sex.

I sat down across from him as he opened a drawer in his desk and took out a bottle of Johnny Walker Blue. He poured a shot for himself and offered me one, but I politely refused.

"I gather everything went well last night?"

"Wonderful!" He shot down the whiskey. It wasn't even seven o'clock.

"I wasn't aware that you knew them. A little heads up would have helped."

"Ha! Like you need help. They loved your presentation and they have only one condition, but they were adamant about it. They want Maggie in any commercials we shoot and in all the magazine and newspaper ads we run."

"You've got to be kidding!"

"They're in love with that girl. What, did she give them all blow jobs before I came down?"

I didn't answer. I was in a state of shock as I watched Jack pour himself another shot.

"You fucking her all day must have given her that extra glow. Guys find that attractive in women."

"She's supposed to start her vacation today. She's off for four weeks."

"That's fine, just tell her not to gain any weight. If anything, tell her to lose a few pounds. You know how the camera adds a few. I was figuring on at least a month before we start shooting and running ads. Is everything okay, Joe?"

"Yeah, everything is great. I imagine she'll be overjoyed."

"Great! Maybe you two can work out a schedule that allows you to hook up before each shoot. Why take a chance? Don't want that glow to disappear."

The phone rang. Jack picked it up and I could hear a woman on the other end with a Russian accent. I took that as my cue to leave.

It was a lie that Maggie was on vacation. She simply wasn't going to be around for a month. I had plans for her, and none of those plans included sunbathing or drinking margaritas.

I stopped at her desk and for the first time ever I infringed upon her privacy. I opened drawer after drawer, and there buried under a stack of files was a bag containing a bunch of little white pills, just as George had described. She was so gone last night that she forgot to take them home. Being a gentleman, I decided to drive over to her house and hand them to her in person.

There are con artists, like colonies of ants, spread throughout Los Angeles. They are vultures, but even a vulture knows when to stop chewing on a corpse. What this con artist had done to Maggie was beyond reprehensible. He not only took all her money but also left her addicted to a deadly drug, a mother with two young children. I would see to it that the miscreant would pay dearly for his misdeeds. Naturally, I would outsource the job to real professionals. I was adamant about hiring the very best. It was the only way I could ever guarantee the desired results.

Chapter Eleven

I parked in Maggie's driveway, knocked on the front door, and was greeted by the lovely nanny who started screaming at me in Spanish. I handed her a couple of hundred-dollar bills, and suddenly she was speaking perfect English and quickly hurried off to wake up the lady of the house.

I walked into the kitchen and sat down at the table. I waited for a good half hour before Maggie appeared in a bathrobe. She looked terrible and nearly stumbled over a kitchen chair as she tried to walk over to the stove and pour herself some coffee. I grabbed onto her and sat her down then poured the coffee for her.

"What are you doing here?" Her voice was barely audible.

"Did you forget I drove you home last night? Your car's back at work."

"Oh yeah." Her hands were trembling as she reached for the coffee. "Wow! I didn't realize how much I had to drink."

"You didn't have anything to drink yesterday, Maggie. You can stop pretending now. I know about everything … the drugs, the pig who took all your money, everything."

"What, are you here to fire me?"

"Please, Maggie, you know me better than that. But it hurts that you didn't come to me for help and that I had to learn all this from someone else."

"I was ashamed, Joe." She looked down into the steaming mug.

"I know, but I thought we promised each other that if either of us got into trouble, we would go to the other for help and advice."

She kept her head and eyes down, staring blankly into what appeared to be oblivion. I reached over and lifted her chin to look into her bleary eyes. "It's time to make it all right again. Go upstairs and clean up. We have a lot to do today."

"I need to stop by the office and pick something up that I left behind last night."

I pulled out the bag of pills. "These?"

"I need just one, please."

I handed her a pill and she swallowed it down with the coffee. She got up from her chair and started to walk up the stairs to her bedroom. I followed. I had a terrible feeling that she might try something stupid, and there was no way I was going to take a chance.

I told her to leave the bathroom door open while she took a shower. I watched as she closed the shower door and turned on the water. Against a tidal wave of water, I could hear her crying violently.

While she got dressed, I got out a suitcase and started packing her underwear, clothes, shoes, toiletries, and other accessories. She pointed to drawers and a closet so I would know where to grab what she needed.

"My children, what about them?"

"They'll be taken care of. When you start feeling better, I'll bring them over to see you. They'll be happy to get their mommy back."

I emptied all of Maggie's mail into a shopping bag, and I told her I'd take care of all the bills. I handed the nanny a few hundred dollars more and told her what I expected from her while Maggie was gone, making it clear that there would be plenty more money coming her way.

I put Maggie's suitcase in the trunk, helped with her seatbelt, and drove to the bank where Maggie had taken out the loan against her house. We sat with a loan officer who took out the paperwork, added the accrued interest and late fees, and came up with a final total of $331,223. Luckily, I had my savings account in the same bank, and in a matter of minutes the funds were transferred to pay off the entire loan. I then opened a new joint account in both our names and put in $50,000.

We got back into my car and Maggie said, "I will never be able to pay you back."

"Funny, you're the second person to tell me that today. Have I ever asked you for anything back? This is not a loan, Maggie. This is family taking care of family. I only ask that you get better." She hugged me, and I kissed her on the cheek.

We went to Gladstone's in Malibu for lunch. Maggie was getting edgy and I gave her one more pill from the bag. It would be the last one she would ever take. We ordered a bottle of wine, crab appetizers, and lobster for our main dishes. I told her about the Japanese executives and how they insisted in the contract that she be in all the commercials and print advertising. She laughed and laughed. I said this might be the beginning of whole new career for her, one that paid a lot of money.

We drove farther up the coast and I pulled into the driveway of The Malibu Rehabilitation Center for Drug and Alcohol Abuse. It was regarded as one of the best treatment centers in the world. I got Maggie's suitcase out of the car and we registered at the desk. An uneasy silence hung between us as we waited for an attendant to take Maggie to her room.

I dropped the bag of pills into a trash can outside the building and drove back home. I had let Maggie down, taken advantage of her at a most frightening time, and hadn't noticed or refused to notice the apparent signs of distress. No amount of money I threw at her now would alleviate the pain I had caused or the guilt that consumed me.

I opened the door to my house at exactly five o'clock. I emptied the shopping bag full of bills onto the kitchen table, grabbed my checkbook, and opened a bottle of red wine. All the bills were overdue and all the credit cards were maxed out. It took me nearly three hours to finish. I paid everything off, put stamps on at least twenty-five envelopes, and walked to the closest mailbox to deposit them. I could have easily waited until the morning and dropped them off on my way to work. The letters weren't going anywhere this late at night, but I just couldn't wait. I had to get them in a mailbox tonight, or else I might go crazy with anxiety.

I walked back home. It was another beautiful southern California night. Couples were out walking and holding hands, others were walking pets, and I was wondering what the hell I was doing here … a place so distant and foreign from where I grew up.

I opened a second bottle of red wine, poured myself a glass, sat down on the couch in the living room, and listened to Sinatra. I was sound asleep when the phone rang at three o'clock in the morning. My first instinct before picking up the phone was that something had gone seriously wrong with Maggie. Phone calls in the middle of the night were never good. I picked the phone up and it was Nancy on the other end. She just wanted to let me know that she got a lovely room, was sleeping alone, and had a wonderful time listening to the speakers at the convention.

I didn't bother asking the obvious question, "What the hell are you doing calling me at this hour?" That would have played right into her hands. I told her that I was also sleeping alone and that there were no guests lingering around. I knew that was the reason she was calling at this ungodly hour, but I kept my cool and was just grateful that she had followed my advice.

Chapter Twelve

Maggie wasn't allowed visitors for the first two weeks at the rehab center, but since I would be driving that way to pick up Nancy at the airport, I figured I would try to bribe my way in. The week had passed relatively quickly, with few problems. It was eerie looking out my office window and seeing a substitute secretary in Maggie's chair. I took comfort in the fact that Maggie would be back there in no time, unless she decided to pursue an acting career once she found out how much money she could make as the face of the Japanese auto company.

True to form, Nancy called every night at three in the morning, but I acted like it didn't bother me. This morning at six I also got a call from her, reminding me to pick her up at the airport, like I could forget.

A couple of hundred-dollar bills to a caretaker smoking a cigarette in the parking lot got me in to see Maggie. I had to climb over bushes and a four-foot-high wall, but it was worth the adventure. "Fifteen minutes," the caretaker warned me several times. I'm pretty sure I could have bought an extra fifteen minutes for a few hundred more.

Maggie was sitting at a desk writing out cards. I knocked gently on the sliding-glass door and she looked up, smiling broadly. In just a few days, I could see a marked improvement. Her complexion, which was usually flawless before her recent misadventures, was almost back to normal. Her eyes were alive again. She hugged me tightly, thanked me profusely, and started asking about her children. Yes, she was on her way to a full recovery, and this time I would be there for her, to help make sure there would be no relapses. If that made Nancy uncomfortable, too bad.

Chapter Thirteen

Picking up the most beautiful girl in the world at the airport would usually bring a huge smile to my face, but there was so much more to my lovely Nancy. The annoying calls in the middle of the night, to a less knowledgeable and giddy guy, might have been seen as proof that she was serious about the relationship, but I knew that she was just insanely jealous of all the other beautiful girls in Los Angeles.

To take the edge off Nancy's arrival, I bought a gram of cocaine. It was a pleasure I occasionally indulged in, but I wasn't a regular user of the garbage. Ironic, after just visiting a rehab center, but what the hell? For the moment, this seemed like my new normal.

I parked across from the terminal, took a hit, and walked to baggage claim. I immediately spotted Nancy at the carousel, her head buried in one of those Russian novels I had given her. I walked up to her and gently tapped her on the shoulder. She turned, smiled, and threw her arms around me, kissing me with such force that I nearly fell over another passenger.

I placed Nancy's luggage, which weighed at least double what it did before she left, in the trunk of the car. I got into the driver's seat, grabbed Nancy's book out of her hand, and flung it into the back seat. After the initial welcome kiss, she had continued to read the book as we walked across the parking garage and got into the car.

"So, did you miss me?" She asked.

"Yes."

"A whole bunch?"

"Yes."

"Great!" she replied, reaching for the book, but I blocked her path.

"Don't make me throw it out, Nancy. I see you didn't work on your etiquette while you were off sunbathing in the desert."

"Funny! If you didn't want me to read the books, you shouldn't have given them to me."

"I hoped they would distract you enough so that you wouldn't go off and screw the first guy who offered to buy you dinner." I sighed, not quite believing what had just come out of my mouth. I waited for a witty reply, but she was quiet.

I desperately needed another hit of coke. I was getting edgy, but there was no way I would do anything in front of her.

I came to a stop at Century Boulevard and waited for what seemed like an eternity for the light to turn green. I switched lanes and got onto the 405 heading east, toward the 101, back to the Valley. I was not going to apologize.

"So you're protective of me; that's sweet, Joe."

I looked at her and realized she wasn't being sarcastic. "I promised you I would be faithful and I keep my promises, but I guess a little bit of jealousy never hurt a relationship. I'm kind of flattered."

"Are you hungry?"

"Yes, but am I going to have to put out first?"

We entered the Smokehouse and were seated right away. I excused myself and went to the bathroom, closed the door to a stall, and snorted two large hits of coke. At the sink on the way out I looked in the mirror for any residue around my nose.

I sat back down at the table and watched Nancy scribble some incomprehensible formula on a piece of paper. I picked up the bottle of wine she had ordered and poured myself a glass. While scribbling with one hand, she was eating a piece of their famous cheesy bread with the other.

Suddenly, I didn't mind that she was ignoring me. The renewed effects of the coke and the taste of the wine were all I needed. Looking at her was more than enough to keep a smile on my face. Or was it?

Nancy moved closer to me and whispered quietly, "I'm working on a formula for a smart bomb. It's going to make me rich, but more importantly, it's going to save millions of lives."

"A smart bomb?" I wasn't quite sure I'd heard her correctly. "Is that anything like a laser-guided missile?"

"Much more advanced than that." She waved her hand, as if to dismiss my comparison as misinformed. "It's a bomb designed with genetic markers to distinguish between the bad guys and the innocent."

"And what type of explosive differentiates between the two?"

"No explosives, just simple radiation that will leave all structures intact and kill only the bad guys."

"That is the stupidest fucking thing I've ever heard. Like the fallout won't kill thousands of innocent people?"

She pulled back from me, her blue eyes like two deadly lasers.

"You know what your problem is, Joe? You can't see beyond that box of lies you and your colleagues have created."

The waitress came over to take our dinner order. I ordered prime rib, medium rare, and Nancy ordered a steak, blood rare. I downed my glass of wine and once again excused myself to take another hit of coke.

It was suddenly all clear to me. New Mexico, deserts, atomic explosions, radioactive sand, tunnels burrowed deep inside mountains, mutant scavengers … A convention, my ass! More like a gathering of the severely deranged — a cult of lunatics with Nancy as the high priestess. And to think that I had been hoping for some normalcy after the nightmare with Maggie. How totally naïve to expect normal from a woman who was clearly batshit crazy.

I sat back down at the table and was somewhat relieved that Nancy had put away her notes and was cutting into her steak.

"I didn't think you were ever coming back." She put a piece of bloody steak into her mouth. I ordered another bottle of wine as I watched her eat and occasionally scribble some formula in the air with her fork.

"It's not going to stay warm much longer, Joe." She pointed to prime rib in front of me.

"That's okay, I like my meat cold."

The waitress filled our glasses from the new bottle. I took a large gulp and finally cut into the meat.

"I'm fairly certain that I can get all the materials I need to build the bomb. Of course, I'll need a secure storage area."

"Wouldn't want any of that radioactive material to leak out, would we?"

She looked at me like my level of stupidity was astonishing. "I'm going to need financing. I already have a few backers. Would you like to contribute? A million or two would surely help."

"I'm sorry, but most of my money is tied up in stocks and it wouldn't be wise for me to sell right now."

"That's funny, I never heard you mention stocks."

"That's because you hate talking about such trivial things as money. It's easier to take mine. When you think about it, we haven't known each other very long. There are lots of things we don't know about each other yet. By the way, can I please have my credit card back?"

She reached into her purse and took out the credit card, but as she went to hand it to me she suddenly paused. "Are you sure? I wanted to buy dinner tonight."

I grabbed the card. "Now what type of gentleman would I be if I let a lady pay?"

I ordered an after-dinner drink, a Johnnie Walker Blue in a warm snifter. Nancy didn't like scotch and scoffed at my suggestion that she order a cordial. She had taken out her pad and pen and was once again writing down bizarre formulas and equations. I swirled the scotch around in the glass and tried to concentrate on her exotic beauty instead of the mutant brain that seemed to be in full possession of her.

Chapter Fourteen

True to form, I took Nancy home and we ripped each other's clothes off. We had crazy sex that went on forever on her cluttered bed. Crazy in the sense that every time I looked at her, she seemed to be calculating some theory in her head, occasionally letting out an unconvincing moan or groan. As for me, between all the coke and booze, I couldn't go on any longer. After about a half hour that seemed like two hours, I rolled off her and apologized for not being able to finish. She didn't seem to care, and to my total surprise, asked me for some cocaine.

"I didn't think you used the stuff."

"I usually don't, but I've been looking at different stimuli that can enhance my staying power and allow me to have longer, more productive days."

I handed her the vial and she sniffed up almost all the rest of the coke. I warned her to be careful, but she waved off my suggestion with a flick of her wrist. "If you plan on staying, please order a lot more." She put on a robe and got up off the bed.

Her apartment was a total disaster. Books were piled precariously high and in no particular order. Never in my life did I imagine I could be buried in an avalanche of books. Newspapers, magazines, pamphlets, and discarded notes were everywhere. The place was dark and eerie, with cobwebs dangling from every corner. The only picture on the walls showed an atomic explosion with this inspirational phrase: DREAM BIG OR NOT AT ALL.

In the bathroom, I had to remove a stack of books piled on the toilet seat before using it. There were books in the shower and in the sink next to splotches of toothpaste and cosmetic products.

I made a call to my dealer, and in less than fifteen minutes he delivered four grams of coke. Before I even closed the door, she grabbed a bag from me, took two large hits, and placed the bag on her desk.

"Is there anything to drink?" I asked.

"Look in the refrigerator."

I opened the door and all I found were cheap wine coolers that I would have been ashamed to serve to drunks living in cardboard boxes. "Don't you have anything else?"

"No! Budget, remember?"

I called a local liquor store and had them deliver a case of quality wine. She finished the first bag of coke before the wine arrived. She didn't say a word as she worked on her crazy theories. I poured her a glass of wine, and she drank it straight down like it was a glass of water. I cleared space on the couch and sat down across from her. "Are you just going to sit there and work on your theories all night?" She picked up a book titled *Glamorous Girls of Hollywood* and flung it at me.

"Why don't you look through that? When you're sufficiently aroused, you can fuck me. But this time from behind, because I can't let this moment of total clarity slip by. I can't afford to have my concentration disturbed."

"How romantic! And what a wonderful use of your valuable time."

"Can I have some more coke?"

"No! You're rude."

"Why would you say that? I let you fuck me, and, according to my mathematical calculations, you're not the greatest lover I've ever had."

"Sorry, next time I'll try harder."

"What makes you think there will be a next time if you don't give me more coke?"

I got up from the couch, turned her chair around, and shook her. "What the hell is wrong with you, Nancy? You're working on a design to build an atomic bomb that you plan on selling. Don't you realize the destructive nature of these weapons? They can kill millions of innocent people. It's absolutely insane to think you can genetically program the bomb to kill only the bad guys."

"I would never sell my bomb to anyone who might use it to kill civilians."

"And why would anyone buy your bomb unless they planned on using it for nefarious purposes? It's not something you place on the mantel of your fireplace, for God's sake."

"I could sell it to Israel. I'm Jewish. They'd probably give me a medal."

"They don't need your bomb — and if they find out a nut like you is building a bomb, they'll most likely have Mossad pay you a visit. And it won't be a friendly visit to pin a medal on you."

She started to cry and went on a rampage, ripping every piece of paper she could get her hands on, throwing books across the room, and turning over her blackboard. I tried to take cover as she took an unabridged, hardcover edition of the Bible and slammed it down on my head.

"You heathen, you filthy disgusting heathen!" she screamed as she punched and kicked me. Finally, she stopped and looked at the framed picture of the atomic explosion. She took it down, slammed it against the desk, and sent glass flying across the room. She discarded it with a fling of her hand. "Satisfied, you son of a bitch?"

"How about a few more hits to cheer you up?"

She grabbed another bag out of my hand. "Thanks."

I couldn't stay in her apartment a moment longer. The place was a disaster before she went crazy, but now it was too much for me to handle. Until recently it was difficult for me to associate a beautiful girl like Nancy with such filth and waste. The few windows in her place were completely covered in black drapes that I imagine she got from the wardrobe department at the studio. I guess she didn't want anyone to see her bomb design and steal it.

Chapter Fifteen

At my insistence, we left her apartment and started walking back to my home in Studio City. The sun was coming up, and like a tidal wave it washed away the stench and odor of Nancy's apartment. I carried the wine and she held onto the coke. She still wore her robe with nothing on underneath, and her tits were on show. I asked her to please cover herself up, and, true to form, she gave me a lecture on the biological function of women's breasts and how our stuck-up, Judeo-Christian morals were responsible for more women getting raped in the United States than in any other civilized country in the world.

I told her to save it for the police when they picked her up for indecent exposure and found all that coke on her. She laughed and took another hit in the middle of the street then offered me some. I looked around, saw no one around, and took a couple of bumps. After all, I had to be on the same plane as this lunatic or else I might kill her.

"I saw one of your disgusting commercials for some oil company on TV; that company is responsible for killing all the wildlife off the coast of Alaska. How do you live with yourself? The way you distort the truth and paint a rosy picture of the cleanup, and with that music in the background? 'What a Wonderful World.' Really? For whom? You and the oil company? Not for the poor ducks and dolphins, that's for sure."

"It helps pay the bills and allows me to take you out to fancy restaurants."

"Oh, please, what you spend on me is mere pittance compared to what you make. You act so self-righteous when passing judgment on me and my design for a bomb, yet you have no problem peddling products like tobacco that kill millions of people each year. At least if my bomb got into the wrong hands, the suffering would end immediately — but with your cancer-causing products that you so happily sell, the suffering goes on for years before the end comes."

"I'm not forcing you to go out to dinner. If my job is so offensive to you, you could always say no."

"And then who would you have to talk to at dinner?"

"I'm sure there must be another girl or two out there nearly as crazy and entertaining as you."

"Really! Who looks like me and is so willing to spread her legs?"

"That's your choice."

"Like I have a choice? All through dinner you stared at my breasts like a hungry tiger."

"Nancy, not that it's any of my business, but how many men have you been with?"

"You're right, it's none of your business, but if I had to guess, around a hundred."

"Holy shit! You're only twenty-four."

"Oh, don't act so coy with me, Joe. You little guinea bastards are barely out of your mothers' wombs before you're trying to screw the first woman you can get your hands on. That's why you Italians are such great lovers; you start so young."

"I thought you said I wasn't much of a lover?"

"True, just my luck, I end up with the reject of the bunch."

"Very nice, Nancy."

"Just telling it the way it is. Sorry, I haven't mastered the art of lying quite as well as you. Next time we do it, I'll try to moan a little more if that makes you happy."

She sat with her robe totally undone on the only sidewalk in the residential area of Studio City. The sun was slowly rising over the one- and two-story homes; in the distance a sign for Universal Studio had become visible. I tried to tie her robe but she pushed my hands away.

"Nancy, you are seriously testing your luck. Some housewife is going to look out her living-room window and see a totally naked woman sitting across from where her children play. She's going to call the police and you are going to have a tough time explaining…"

"If you're that frightened, just leave! God forbid if the sterling reputation of Joe Rossetti was soiled in any way."

I lifted her head and looked into her eyes, glazed and glassy from the booze and coke, yet still penetrating. I felt guilty for mocking her dream. She had apparently put a lot of thought and effort into building this bomb. I took her hand. "Nancy, please, I don't want anything to happen to you. Let's get out of here, go back to my place, and you can scream and rant all you want."

She tied her robe and took my hand. Finally, we made it back to my house and celebrated by listening to Pink Floyd's *Dark Side of the Moon*. We dumped the remaining coke on the album cover. It made an impressive mountain of white powder but didn't last long. Nancy did not practice self-control when it came to this stuff. Then again, who did? Thankfully, the "drugstore" was open 24/7, and I placed another order that was delivered promptly.

Nancy was in a much better mood after that, and, even though Floyd's music didn't exactly conjure up a desire to go out on the dance floor, she was nevertheless dancing naked around the house … Who was I to complain? After the album finished, she sat beside me, picked up the straw on the table, and took two more hits. She crossed her legs, picked up her glass of wine, and looked at me like a psychologist studying a sick and deranged patient.

"Feeling better?" I asked.

"Much! Sorry I was gloomy before. It's not easy to give up something I've been working on so diligently for so long."

"And sacrificing so much. At least now you'll have enough money to buy better-quality liquor. How much did you actually save?"

"A few hundred."

"A few hundred thousand?"

"No, silly, a few hundred dollars."

It was hard, but I kept my mouth shut. Nancy made plenty of money — nothing like what I made — but plenty. She was well respected and exceptional at her job. I bent down and took two giant hits of the coke.

"Can I tell you a secret?"

"Of course."

"Of all the men I have been with, and a few women, you are the only one I have seriously thought of introducing to my mother."

"And why is that?"

"Because you are the only one I have seriously thought of marrying. Sure, you have your shortcomings, but you're very handsome, rich, generous, protective, and fairly intelligent. And you're Italian and Catholic."

"And why would that matter?"

"Because statistics show that Italian Catholics are a lot less likely to get divorced. That doesn't mean you wouldn't be any less likely to cheat, but at the end of the night you will always come back home."

"Interesting!"

"My father raped me for the first time when I was fourteen."

"What?"

"He first raped me at fourteen and repeatedly thereafter until I left home at sixteen. And what was my mother doing while this was taking place? She was cooking dinner and watching *The Dick Van Dyke Show* on a black-and-white TV in the kitchen."

"Did you tell her what was going on?"

"Of course! She said it was all in my imagination, and I should be ashamed to make such false accusations."

"You're kidding!"

"No, Joe, I'm not kidding. She also said I shouldn't wear such provocative outfits; it was unbecoming for a young lady, and I was only asking for trouble."

"And this is the woman you want to introduce me to?"

"She's changed. She has dementia and doesn't recognize anyone or remember anything."

I felt Nancy falling back into her earlier gloomy mood, so I recommended she take a few more hits, which she quickly did. She then walked over to my record recollection and started going through all my albums. "You have wonderful taste in music, Joe. I imagine it's a great inspiration to you when you sit down and put together an advertising campaign, peddling a bunch of lies to the uneducated and gullible masses."

"It certainly helps." She put on a Frank Sinatra album.

"Dance with me, Joe."

"First you need to put on some clothes; otherwise there's going to be a huge bulge separating us, and after all the coke I don't know if I'm up to the challenge."

Nancy walked into my bedroom, opened the door to my closet, and put on another one of my Armani sport coats. It was naturally, again, way too big for her, but my God, she was hot.

"Are you trying to kill me?"

I spun her around and we danced cheek to cheek to Ol' Blue Eyes, with an occasional dip.

"I haven't paid my rent in two months. How many months can you usually go without being thrown out?"

"I think it's three. You need to move out of there. The place is a dump. Do you even have air conditioning?"

"I used to have a window unit, but one night when I was working on my design for the bomb, I got so frustrated that I kicked it straight out the window. Thank God nobody was walking by."

"They just finished building new condominiums about half a mile from here. They look really nice and in a safe, beautiful area. You should look at them."

"And where would I get the down payment?"

"I'll give you the down payment."

"Well, if you're going to do that, why don't you just buy the place for me outright? Then I wouldn't have to worry about any paym

"They're going for eighty thousand dollars. Isn't that askin
much?"

"Isn't that less than you make in a month?"

"Yeah, usually."

"And it's not like you have a family to support. You don't even have a dog or a cat, and I know this house is paid for."

"You make good money. I don't understand for the life of me why you never have any."

"Life is expensive, and what you make in a month, I don't make in a year."

"We'll go take a look at the condos in two weeks when they have their first open house."

"And you're going to pay for the whole thing?"

"I'll sleep on it."

"Joe, why don't you just marry me? You know you're crazy about me, and I'm the most fascinating and appealing thing in your life. Then we won't have to waste money on some condo."

It was impossible to deny. She was the most exciting and stimulating woman I'd ever met. Perplexing, frustrating, even irritating at times, but from the moment I set eyes on her I was in awe. Drop-dead gorgeous, off-the-charts brilliant, unpredictable, fearless, and for some crazy reason we were better together than apart. It didn't hurt that she was reading my favorite novels one by one. Granted, the pages of those books would never be the same after her frenzied scribbles in every bit of free space, but I had come to appreciate that she devoured books the way she did a piece of red meat, a bag of cocaine, or me.

"If you don't mind me asking, whatever happened to your father?"

"I cut his dick off while he was asleep, drunk. I locked the door to his room and he bled to death. It was ruled a suicide."

We continued dancing, occasionally stopping to powder our noses and drink some wine. We eventually took the party outside and sat by the pool. Nancy decided to take a dip. It was hot, and all the coke only magnified the heat. I watched her walk to the edge of the diving board, and I swear at that moment I had never seen a girl so beautiful and sexy. She dove into the water without bothering to take off my coat. She swam the length of the pool and stepped out, dripping wet, my $400 jacket ruined, and walked up to me.

"Did you enjoy?" she giggled.

"Quite amazing!"

She took the jacket off and dropped it in a garbage can I kept outside. I threw her a towel and she dried herself off. "Do you mind if I put on another one of your jackets? I so love Armani!"

"Only if you promise to let me know when you plan on taking another dip, so I can take a picture and have the memory forever frozen in time."

In the end, life is a series of moments. No one knew that better than I did, and no one was better at creating memorable moments than Nancy.

At ten o'clock that night we ran out of coke and debated whether we should order more. Wisdom won and we took two sleeping pills each, drank another bottle of wine, and passed out on the bed watching *All About Eve.*

Chapter Sixteen

After ten wonderful hours of sleep, I found my lovely Nancy sitting at my desk reading Sunday's *Los Angeles Times* and, as usual, taking notes. Discarded pieces of the paper were strewn all over the place. She was concentrating so deeply that she didn't hear me get out of bed and walk toward her. I bent down and whispered in her ear, "Sleep well?" She looked up and smiled, "Wonderfully, Joe."

She was drinking a glass of wine and offered me some, which I gladly accepted. She reached for a list and handed it to me. "A recap of yesterday and all the promises you made to me." At the very top of the list in bold was the promise to buy her a condo and pay for the entire thing. Just below that, she wrote, "But the wise thing to do, as we discussed, is simply to marry me, save the money on the condo, and live a happy and crazy life forever and ever with the girl of your dreams."

She pointed out that she would sign a prenup just in case I thought she was after my money. Even though many other men had begged her to marry them, never once insulting her with the mention of a prenup, I was "too perfect a man to let slip by" without a fight.

Before I could finish reading the recap, Nancy informed me that she was moving in for the next two weeks. When I said I didn't think it was a good idea, she sternly replied, "Yes, it is a good idea. It's the only way you will know what a perfect wife I'll make. Why blow your money on a condo when you can have the best thing in your life living with you all the time?" She decided that I didn't need to meet her mother. "Let the bitch rot looking at reruns of *The Dick Van Dyke Show* believing that Mary Tyler Moore is her child."

I took a large gulp of her wine. I didn't have the mental capacity to argue with her just then. She added that she would not accept just living with me. It was either marriage or the condo. She was willing to compromise and try a 30-day trial period, but that was it. I told her I would think it over. It was a lot to mull over so early in the morning, and I needed a shower.

She informed me that she had already showered and had used my toothbrush, which she didn't see any problem with. After all, we had already passed our germs to each other playing doctor and snorting a mound of coke from the same straw. She offered to cook breakfast, which was almost as big a shock as her ultimatum.

"I didn't know you cooked."

"I don't, but if you're willing to take a risk, so am I."

I told her to order out and have it delivered. She was fine with that.

I walked into the bathroom and found a disaster area. The shampoo and conditioner bottles were on the floor of the shower. Sections of *The Los Angeles Times* were scattered around the toilet. My unrinsed toothbrush was sitting on the edge of the sink. She had apparently used my razor to shave her legs and God knows what else. I cleaned the bathroom as quietly as I could, for some bizarre reason not wanting her to feel self-conscious about the mess she'd made. Why I believed she might be self-conscious about anything I don't know, but in spite of everything it was my nature to be a gentleman. Thankfully, I had a spare toothbrush under the sink. I got in the shower, closed my eyes, and let the cold water pound against my body until I was literally quivering with pain.

I got dressed and left the bathroom just as breakfast was delivered. Nancy was going through my wallet, taking out cash to pay the deliveryman. "Hope you gave him a good tip." She smiled. "I always leave good tips."

She chaotically set the dining-room table with plastic utensils and paper napkins from the delivery bag. She ate a piece of toast with scrambled eggs, and I tore through the six pancakes and six pieces of French toast she had drenched in butter and maple syrup for me. I was starving and ate it all, along with two glasses of wine.

"So did you think over what we discussed?"

"Nope, not yet. We have time."

"If it's no trouble, can you drop me off at my apartment so I can pick up clothes and other things I need for work?"

"No problem."

"We can't stay too long because I don't want to run into the owner and get into a fight, even though he'll probably be happy to hear that I'm leaving."

Nancy finished her breakfast, took the glass of wine, and walked away without clearing any of the remains on the table. "Um, Nancy, sweetheart, did you forget something?" She turned back around and looked at me. "I don't think so." I pointed to her dirty remains from breakfast and said, "There's a garbage can in the kitchen."

"Oh, I'm sorry." She picked up the mess and disappeared into the kitchen, then re-emerged with a full glass and a new bottle of wine. She refilled my glass, remarking, "You see, I can be perfect in so many ways."

We drove back to her apartment a few hours later. The thought of going back into that hellhole was disturbing enough, but as luck would have it, there was a parking space right in front of her complex. We got out of the car and started to walk up the stairs, but I stopped and told her I'd forgotten something in the car. "Fine, just don't be too long."

I walked around to the manager's office, knocked on the door, and walked in. The manager, a slight, effeminate man in his early fifties, looked up from the TV and said, "What can I do for you? We have no vacancies."

"I'm here to pay Nancy's back rent. Apt. 302."

"Seriously, I was planning on kicking that sick bitch out at the end of month."

"That sick bitch is my sister."

"Doesn't make her any less sick."

"How much does she owe?"

"She's three months behind, including this month. So that's $3750."

I paid the man and told him, against my better instincts, that Nancy would be moving out at the end of the month.

"Hallelujah! Hallelujah!"

I entered Nancy's apartment and the place looked even worse than I remembered. She was throwing clothes and books haphazardly into empty cardboard boxes. "Where the hell have you been?"

"I paid your back rent and told the manager you'd be moving out at the end of the month."

"Why?"

"Because it was the right thing to do, Nancy."

"Did you at least get my security deposit back?"

"Nancy, darling, have you ever been spanked?"

"Not that I recall, but who knows, it might be fun. I'm game if you are. Does that type of shit turn you on?"

"No, Nancy, it doesn't, but if you keep it up I'm going to take off my belt."

"Oh, please, you would never hit a woman."

"Not a woman, no, but I'd have no problem whipping a selfish little child like you."

"Screw you!" She handed me a box to carry down to the car.

Chapter Seventeen

Nancy and I carpooled to work or, more correctly, I drove while Nancy changed stations on the radio. The drive was short, not more than a few miles, but it took over a half hour to get to our destinations. Nancy had designed a two-passenger helicopter no bigger than a Volkswagen that would allow travelers the luxury of flying over this nightmarish traffic. It would be very costly to manufacture and crazy expensive to buy; if every jackass could afford one, the traffic nightmare would simply transfer from the ground to the air. What good would that do?

Nancy asked me if I would finance the project. "No!"

"Of course not. Why get involved in anything that might relieve the suffering caused by overpopulation and congestion when you help sell cigarettes? It's cool and sexy, and who doesn't want to cut their life expectancy by at least ten to fifteen years?!"

In a determined effort to prove how truly wonderful she was and what a great wife she would make, Nancy decided that we should have lunch together every day for the next two weeks. I was asked to choose the restaurant since I was, naturally, paying. I chose Mo's Restaurant, a landmark in Toluca Lake. I ate lunch there at least three times a week. Wonderful food, charming atmosphere, and the service was great. I never had to wait for a table even though the place was usually packed. I was a great tipper, and I spread the money around to everyone from the busboy to the maître d'.

I got there about fifteen minutes before Nancy, just enough time to have two hot and spicy Bloody Marys. Needless to say, she was the main attraction from the moment she arrived. In a town with more beautiful girls per square foot than any other place in the world, Nancy was a showstopper. It was as though time stopped when she entered a room.

She sat down across from me and ordered whatever I was drinking. She surveyed the clientele, reached into her pocketbook, and took out a notebook. She wrote a few lines and passed the paper to me. It read, "I could have fifty percent of the men in this restaurant get down on their knees and beg me for a date."

I passed the paper back to her. "Only fifty percent??" She laughed.

"That's accounting for the fact that thirty percent are fags and another twenty percent are depraved perverts who prey on the weak and innocent. This is Los Angeles, after all."

I asked her about work. "Same shit, Joe. Creating magic on the same tired, worn-out faces of spoiled, talentless actresses … making them look a lot more beautiful than they deserve to."

"What keeps you behind the scenes instead of in front of the camera? You could be making a ton more money."

"Would you like me better then? A prized piece of famous ass to showcase?"

"Drop the bullshit, Nancy. I'm working on a national campaign for a new perfume that's going to be huge. The feedback has been over the top. I am talking serious bucks."

"And what makes you think they would want me?"

"Because they listen to me. Or would you rather they hire Bo Derek or some talentless ditz?"

"And how many innocent animals have they killed while testing this wonderful new product?"

I shook my head as the waiter came over to take our order. Nancy ordered a salad with walnuts and Italian dressing, and I ordered a jumbo cheeseburger with an extra order of fries.

"I appreciate the offer, Joe, but I'm too busy working on other things."

"Like avoiding your landlord so he won't ask you for the back rent?"

"That's been put to rest, as you well know. I'm starting a new chapter in my life. You're looking at the best and most honest thing in your otherwise deceitful life. It's about time you open your eyes and stop looking at only my tits, face, and ass."

"You know damn well that's not all I look at. Your legs and hair are also marvelous, not to mention the back of your neck."

"You're a real ass."

"Maybe so, but if I have anything to say — and I do — you are going to be the face of this new perfume. So when we get home tonight, be ready to take some sexy pictures wearing one of my Armani sport coats you're so fond of."

"That reminds me, can you drive me downtown to the library after work?"

"I'll just buy you the books. It'll be a lot less frustrating than trying to get downtown during rush-hour traffic."

"They're not the type of books you can buy in any bookstore. They're research books, and only the library downtown has them."

"Should I even ask what you're researching?"

"I'll tell you later; too many people are around."

"Should I be concerned?"

"Only if you're a sexual pervert."

The waiter came with our food, and I ordered another Bloody Mary. Nancy asked for an iced tea.

After lunch, I walked Nancy back to the studio. My day was almost over, except for a little fine-tuning, which I could easily do at the Smokehouse bar.

Nancy's new research involved developing a pill, or even better, a spray, that would cause sudden, painful, and temporary genital paralysis in male predators. She was already working with a chemist. She said she needed to go to the library to research the work on castration the Nazis had performed on human subjects. I told her the whole thing seemed unethical, especially since she was Jewish.

She first replied that she was appalled both as a human being and a Jew, but then it occurred to her that, at times, scientists had to plunge into the very pit of humanity's inhumanity to cure illness.

"That sounds like a rationalization: justifying cruelty as a means to an end."

"It's not like I can undo the past. What greater honor to the victims of the Holocaust than to know they didn't die in vain? Maybe if *your* parent raped you repeatedly as a child, you would think differently. *Your* parent..." she repeated again and again, pounding on my chest with her hand. I was exactly the type of person she was trying to protect innocent women against — young, rich, handsome men who thought they were God's gift to the world and a woman's body was just something to be used for their pleasure and then discarded.

She let out a long sigh as she turned to the crowd that had gathered around us. "And what the hell are you bunch of perverts looking at?" They scattered like flies. I, on the other hand, tried to remain calm and concentrate on how wonderful that first cold beer at the Smokehouse was going to taste.

Nancy took my hand and, like a five-year-old child, I followed. "I seriously hope you don't hold this against me when you evaluate our relationship at the end of the two weeks. I think it would be very foolish of you if you did."

I pretended I didn't know what she was talking about. "What time should I pick you up?"

"I get out at five. If that's too early, I can..."

"No! Five is great."

She kissed me on the cheek and whispered in my ear, "Please don't be mad at me."

I watched as she walked down the hallway of her building and then turned around and headed straight for the Smokehouse. The lunch crowd had departed and except for a few patrons at the bar and a couple at a table, the restaurant was empty. The bartender, Fernando, reached into a bucket of ice and grabbed a Budweiser for me. I guzzled the beer and before I could order another, Fernando had already placed it in front me. We had become friends over the years and usually discussed baseball. He was a big Los Angeles Dodgers fan and I was a New York Yankees fan. Clients were constantly giving me free clubhouse tickets to Dodgers games; I used to give them to Fernando and he would take his family.

Fernando was busy restocking the bar. I took out a notepad I carried with me at all times and turned to a clean page. I drew a line down the middle of the page; the left side I titled "Pros" and the right side "Cons." At the very top of the page I wrote Nancy's name.

Pro #1: She's so stunning, she could melt the sun.

Con #1: She's so stunning, I often can't see past it.

Pro #2: She's exceptionally intelligent and has a wide range of knowledge. She is unpredictable and creative and can show an alarming level of concentration.

Con #2: She might unknowingly use any of those attributes one day to help destroy the planet.

Pro #3: She has morals, and, despite her sudden outbursts, she has a conscience and a real concern for humanity. Excluding her latest fascination with Nazi research and building a bomb, Nancy is the only person I've met in this town who doesn't lie to further her own agenda.

Con #3: At times, I think she uses me as her personal lab rat to prove or discredit her theories and experiments.

Pro #4: She is unique…

I stopped writing at that point, pulled the sheet from the pad, crumpled it into a ball, and threw it into the wastebasket behind the bar. I had a few more beers, left a fifty on the bar, and told Fernando I'd see him in a day or two.

I went back to my office and the temporary secretary handed me ten messages. My God, how I missed my precious Maggie, but she would be back soon enough. Eight of the messages were from Nancy, and two were from the perfume company I was working with. A few famous actresses had expressed interest in representing the company. They were all hot and would be perfect for the campaign, but none of them as much as Nancy. I called the company back and told them I had one more potential candidate in mind and she was even better than the stars who had already been considered. I said I'd send pictures in the next day or two and that she would not disappoint. They had total faith in my judgment.

I called Nancy back and she asked where I had disappeared to.

"I was in a meeting."

"With who, the bartender at the Smokehouse?"

I didn't bother to reply, instead jumping to the more important issue. "I just told the perfume executives about you. They're excited, so be ready to take some sexy photos tonight wearing my Armani sport coats you so love."

It was her turn not to answer. She jumped right to the reason she had called eight times. "I can get out at four, so if you're not too busy with any more meetings, we can drive to the library before the traffic gets totally crazy."

Chapter Eighteen

I was outside her building a little before four, got out of the car to stretch my legs, and waited on the passenger side. Nancy came a few minutes later carrying an expensive leather Coach briefcase. I opened the door for her and she replied with a sexy, "Thank you kindly, sweet sir."

I walked back to the driver's side and climbed in, and, before I had time to close the door, she had her lips pressed tightly against mine, her tongue halfway down my throat, and her hands all over my body. I literally had to push her off of me. "What the hell is that about?"

"Just saying hello. Complaining, are you?"

I closed the door as she reached over and grabbed my erect penis.

"You keep it up, and we'll never make it to the library."

She pulled away, reached into her briefcase, and pulled out a spray bottle. "You disgusting pig!" With that she sprayed me in the face with something that smelled like urine.

"What the hell—?"

"Oh, don't be such a baby. Just a little demonstration of the power of the product I'm working on."

"What did you just spray in my face?"

"A drop of my urine mixed with water. Nothing that will do you any harm, not like the finished product." She touched my penis again, which had understandably gone limp. "You see, it works."

"Please tell me you're joking."

"I'm not joking. It's not like you haven't tasted my urine before. After all, how many times have you gone down on me?"

I felt sick as she sprayed some in her hand and exclaimed, "Wow! That does stink. What was in that salad I had for lunch?"

I got out of the car, walked into the building, and entered the first bathroom I saw. I washed my face over and over again but still couldn't get rid of the smell. I finally gave up, went back to the car, and started driving.

"Don't say another word!" I yelled as I started driving toward the library. The traffic on the freeway was terrible. Her idea that it would be any better because we left an hour earlier was insane. This was Los Angeles, for God's sake, the only place on earth where you can run into heavy traffic at three in the morning on a five-lane freeway!

"Do you think your mom would like me if she was still alive?"

"What type of question is that after you just sprayed piss in my face?"

"Oh, get over it! I thought boys from the Bronx were supposed to be tough, not little crybabies. Now, back to the question ... do you think your mother would like me?"

"Yeah, if you didn't open your mouth, she would probably think you were the most beautiful woman she had ever seen, but once you did and started talking about your advanced theories on castration and building bombs of mass destruction, she might think you were insane."

"How about if I stuck to the basics, like movies and music?"

"Then she would probably think you were perfect, but really, how long do you honestly think it would take you to change the subject?"

"When you were sitting back there on the park benches in the Bronx, did you dream about a girl like me?"

"How could I possibly dream about a girl like you without her last name being Da Vinci or Einstein?"

"Oh, that's sweet. Thank you, Joe. So tell me, if you were a girl and your mother found out your father was raping you, what would she do?"

"That would never happen."

"I know, but just pretend it did. What would your mother do?"

"She would gut the son of a bitch!"

"That's what I thought."

"Did you really cut off your father's penis?"

"Yes. You know I don't lie."

"Then I don't understand how it was ruled a suicide. Who the fuck cuts off his dick to commit suicide?"

"I told the police what he had been doing to me and they totally believed it. Besides, they both had major crushes on me."

"Don't tell me, you screwed both of them?"

"Yeah, I did. The younger one was really good. He was the first one to make me come without the help of an inanimate object."

"Of course he was."

"Who was the first girl you had sex with, or was that me?"

"Very cute, Nancy."

"It's nothing to be ashamed of. If nothing else, that would explain a lot."

"You know, Nancy, where I come from you don't advertise to the world every girl you've been with."

"That's funny, because you don't have any problem advertising everything else."

"Keep it up, and you just might find your cute little ass on the side of the road."

"Like I would have a problem getting a ride. I could put my thumb up and in less than a minute I'd have cars lining up to take me anywhere I want to go."

"Yeah, but you might not get so lucky. The guy you choose might not be a gentleman. Your spray of piss just might turn him on."

"So what size family are we looking at?"

"Why are you asking me? Shouldn't you be asking the young cop that question? Surely, you want to be married to a man who can satisfy you at that magical moment of conception."

"He's married. I would never break up a family."

"But you had no problem fucking him behind his wife's back. That's real class, Nancy."

"I owed him."

"So you're telling me you're no better than a hooker?"

"Stop it! Don't blame me for your shortcomings. It's not like I get anything out of the deal. I gave you an honest assessment."

"And I just gave you an honest assessment."

"Bullshit. You make a fortune telling lies. If deep down you really thought I was a hooker, you wouldn't have me live with you."

"It's temporary, remember? And why all the maternal urges?"

"I don't have any desire to get pregnant, but I know you wops are all about having children. I thought it would be nice to give you at least one child."

"Wow! That is so thoughtful and unselfish of you."

"Don't be sarcastic. It only makes you sound dumber than you are."

An hour and twenty minutes later, after driving a total of seven miles, we finally arrived at the library. The only good thing was that it was easy to park because all the people leaving work couldn't wait to get the hell out of this part of town. After dark, downtown Los Angeles became a refuge for gangs, drug addicts, and the homeless; no upstanding citizens wanted to be around that crowd.

The library was a tremendous structure; naturally, Nancy took us to a section that had probably not seen a visitor since it opened. I grabbed a cart and Nancy started placing huge reference books in it. She had me roll the cart next to a photocopier then sat down at a table next to the cart. I sat down and watched as she opened a book with gruesome pictures of experiments done on Jews in the concentration camps during World War II. She seemed to view the pictures with little interest and started reading attentively. I got up from my chair and decided to get a normal book to read, but before I got a few feet away she called me back. "Can you please copy these pages I marked?" She pushed the book toward me and I replied, "How about a little money? It costs money to make copies."

She looked at me with disdain. "I thought the pleasure of my company would be enough to cover the price of a few copies."

"You thought wrong."

She reached into her briefcase and took out her wallet. She poured out all the money it contained onto the table. It came to a little over two dollars. "Seriously, that's all the money you have?"

"Sorry, I don't make millions peddling toxins to the downtrodden."

"Drop it, Nancy! How much was that briefcase you're walking around with? About five hundred?"

"It was a gift."

"Of course, for services rendered?"

"You pig!"

"Oh please, stop it. You're selling your greatest asset. I get that. It's smart."

She looked at me for a long moment. "Can you please make me those copies?"

I picked up the two dollars and change and put it in my pocket. I took the book and walked over to the machine. Hurting Nancy was never my intention. Other guys would argue that she deserved a lot worse, but no one else knew her backstory like I did.

Before we were done I had spent over $120 on copies. There had to be more than 1000 pages beside Nancy on the table, and she was beginning to show signs of being upset. The subject matter, the disturbing pictures, and the idea of treating innocent people like lab rats had reawakened the most beautiful thing about Nancy: her unyielding moral compass.

Once in the car, Nancy was unusually quiet as she stared out the passenger window. I decided that the best course of action was to be quiet. It wasn't until we got off the freeway and onto Ventura Boulevard that she said, "It is hard to imagine that one group of people could so dehumanize another simply because of their ethnic and religious background." I reached over and took Nancy's trembling hand. She gripped my hand tightly.

I pulled into the driveway and parked. Nancy left the copies in the car. She said she was too tired to do any more research. We walked into the living room and Nancy flopped down on the couch. She asked me to put on some of Frank Sinatra's old, barroom ballads. When Nancy was depressed, she liked to listen to music that complemented her mood. Sinatra fit all the requirements — the great, unmatched voice, his impeccable timing, and the genuine emotion he put into every word of a song.

I went into the kitchen and poured two large glasses of white wine. When I went back to the living room a minute later, Nancy was out cold. I sat down with the wine and couldn't help wondering if her dreams were actually nightmares; she was so beautiful and brilliant, yet she was clearly haunted by demons I could not imagine.

She found my occupation offensive yet had no problem taking money from me. She was great at her job. Maybe her occupation was a form of sublimation, a desire to correct her own imperfections, a way to address her childhood abuse. At that moment, with Sinatra singing in the background, I pitied the innocent, wounded child across from me. I finished off the wine, put a blanket over Nancy, and went into my bedroom to sleep.

At about three in the morning, Nancy got into bed and nudged me just enough to wake me. "Sorry I fell asleep. I promised you I'd pose for some pictures. Maybe in the morning, before work."

"It's okay. I would never make you do anything that made you feel uncomfortable. I love you."

I could see tears glow in her eyes.

"I could probably use the money," she chokingly replied.

"I can give you money. Stay true to yourself."

She kissed me sweetly and lay her head on my chest. I could feel her tears soak through my T-shirt and rattle the inner sanctum of my soul.

Chapter Nineteen

I could hear Nancy in the shower when I got up the next morning. I got out of bed and gathered all the trash around the house. I took it out back, opened the trashcan, and saw that Nancy had thrown away all the copies of the Nazi experiments. I dumped the trash on top of the copies and put the cover back on.

I walked back into the house as Nancy came out of the bedroom. Her hair was tied back really tight. I had never seen it like that and must have looked a little puzzled at first.

"You don't like it?"

"Just the opposite; you look gorgeous."

"Thank you! I'm going to get paid this week and I'll do my best to try and save a portion."

I didn't know what to say, so I remained quiet as she continued. "And for the record, I did not screw anyone for my Coach briefcase, and there are not now, nor will there ever be, any pending services."

I wasn't exactly sure what was going on, so I still didn't say anything. "I am going to try my hardest to make this work, Joe. I know how much you love me, and last night confirmed that."

She had thrown a number of curveballs my way in the time I'd known her, but this was an unhittable Bert Blyleven curveball. Our relationship was undoubtedly dysfunctional, but it seemed to work for both of us. I loved Nancy and wanted to believe that she loved me, but there were quite a few unresolved issues.

I looked at her and simply said, "That sounds great."

I took a shower and allowed the cold water to splash my face. It didn't help, so I turned the water to a more comfortable temperature.

Chapter Twenty

On the ride to work the next day, Nancy told me she was working on some ideas for that night and would tell me more at lunch. I stopped the car in front of the main entrance to her building, and she reached over and kissed me deeply, passionately. "That's to keep you happy until lunch." She got out of the car, closed the door, and looked back one last time to blow me a kiss. I drove off and went to my office. The temporary secretary asked if I would like some coffee.

"I need something a lot stronger than coffee, but thanks." I entered my office and looked at my bottle of Johnnie Walker Black. I was tempted but thought better of it. It was important to keep a clear head. Nancy was acting dangerously normal, and that was more worrisome than her acting dangerously insane.

I looked through the pictures the perfume company had sent over. The actresses and models were all good choices, but Nancy would have put them all to shame. A golden opportunity, but she had refused to bite and I respected her wishes.

I arrived at Mo's Restaurant fifteen minutes early again, but instead of a Bloody Mary I ordered an iced tea. Nancy walked in shortly after me and also ordered an iced tea. "No Bloody Mary this afternoon?"

"No, trying to cut back."

"Good! I don't want to be married to an alcoholic."

She took out a piece of paper and handed it to me. It was a list of Ingrid Bergman movies. "I remember you telling me you had a major crush on her, and since she's no threat to me I thought we could have an Ingrid festival the rest of this week. We can start tonight with *Gaslight* and *Notorious*, if you like."

"That would be great!"

"Good, I thought you might like it. I'm also going to try cooking tonight. Tell me your favorite dish and I'll make it for you."

I almost choked on an ice cube as I scrambled for an answer. "I was actually thinking Chinese for tonight. We can order in."

"Okay, maybe tomorrow night."

"Wednesday night is always pizza. You know that."

"Okay, then Thursday."

The waiter came over and asked if we were ready to order. "I would like the walnut salad please, but leave out the asparagus. I had it yesterday and my piss smelled something awful." She pointed at me. "You can ask him. He smelled it." I dropped my head in embarrassment. Without looking up, I ordered a double cheeseburger with fries.

Once he walked away, I asked, "Was it really necessary to tell the waiter about the smell of your urine?"

"What's the big deal? It's just pee. Weren't you in the Boy Scouts?"

"No!"

"Really, that explains a lot." She put her hand under her chin like she was examining her latest specimen.

"The great outdoors was right outside our house in the Bronx."

"Really, I didn't know you lived by the Bronx Zoo."

"I didn't."

"Oh, I get it. You're trying to equate the Bronx with the Wild West. Not a very good analogy, Joe. I know for a fact that you come from an Italian-infested area of the Bronx where the crime rate was zero."

"And don't you think I ever went outside that safe zone?"

"I don't know, Joseph, did you?"

"Please don't call me Joseph. You know I don't like to be called that."

She ran her hand through my hair. "Has anyone ever told you that you look like Marcello Mastroianni?"

"No one, not ever."

"That's probably because no one you know has ever seen a Fellini movie. I find him incredibly sexy."

"That's great! Maybe after we're finished with the Ingrid festival, we can start a Marcello festival?"

She whispered, "That would assure you of getting laid at least twice a night, if not three times. You think you're up for that?"

I walked Nancy back to work and just before we got to the door of her building I hugged her tightly, taking her by surprise, and told her how much I loved her and appreciated the effort she was putting into our relationship. She walked into the building, turned, and blew me a kiss. I smiled and waved, turned, and walked quickly to the Smokehouse to talk to Fernando.

Before I even took my place at the half-empty bar, Fernando had a cold Budweiser waiting for me. When he got a moment, we talked about Nancy. He had met her on previous occasions and remembered her instantly. He said, "To honor such beauty, to love such a magnificent woman, meant one of two things for the unlucky suitor: one, a large withdrawal from his bank account; or two, the relinquishing of his soul." Fernando, like so many other bartenders, was a true philosopher.

As a tip I left him $100 and clubhouse tickets to the next Dodgers game. I went back to the office and another bunch of messages. Like the day before, two-thirds of them were from Nancy, but the others were great news. A major car manufacturer I had created an advertising campaign for had finally agreed with my suggestion to use a bestselling song from a Detroit musician in their commercial for a new truck they were rolling out. The musician was on board from the start, but the manufacturer had been skeptical about the cost and the royalties they would have to pay out every time the commercial ran.

(Thirty years later, different versions of the commercial were still running, and the song had become the anthem for every new truck rolled out.)

After I calmed down, I called Nancy and told her about the deal. Her response was curt and cold. "It figures, only you could poison a beautiful song for profit." She hung up without telling me why she'd left eight messages. By the time I picked her up after work, she was back to her Donna Reed impersonation. She didn't mention the song and once again offered to cook dinner. I politely declined, but stopped at a supermarket so she could pick up some microwave popcorn for our movie marathon. She put the bag in the back seat, got back into the car, then told me how happy she was feeling. I braced myself, waiting to hear how her happiness was linked to something I was expected to do.

"I was thinking," she started, "would it be okay if I put my paycheck into your bank account? That way I won't be tempted to spend it all."

"No."

"Just like that? Without giving it any thought at all?"

"That's right, just like that. I don't mix my finances. It's less complicated that way."

"What about after we get married?"

"You don't have a ring on your finger yet, darling, much less a proposal."

She looked hard at me and I could feel the old Nancy about to emerge. "I see," she said bitterly. "I guess it's helpful to know that I'm going to have to put all the work into this relationship if it has any chance at all."

"Not all the work, Nancy. I appreciate you wanting to make some changes and be more responsible financially. To prove it and show my gratitude, I'll match dollar for dollar everything you put into your bank account for the first month."

"How sweet, and what do you get in return? A free pass to fuck me in the ass?"

"I don't go there, you know that. You get my unbridled loyalty."

She sighed heavily as she folded her arms and looked out the window. "Your unbridled loyalty ... does that include your unbridled love? Or is that something different?"

"How many times do I have to tell you how much I love you? How much unconditional support and encouragement do you need to understand that I'm not going anywhere?"

"Oh, don't give me that shit. Lying comes as naturally to you as breathing, and as for the support, that's easy when you have as much money as you do."

"Really? Okay! Why not just go out and pick up another rich guy? I'll understand, and after he's tired of fucking you and kicks you out, I'll be here waiting for you. How's that for loyalty? Just don't bring back any diseases."

"You arrogant motherfucker!"

"Atta girl ... that's the sweet ray of sunshine any guy would be happy to introduce to his mother."

"I might be alone in this world, but if I am sure of anything, you are even more alone. Aren't you?"

"Maybe, but I'm fairly confident that I have the capacity to make friends. That's more than I could say for you."

She shook her head and started tapping the window with her nails. "At least I can look in the mirror and know I'm true to myself."

"That's wonderful, but it doesn't pay the bills."

She turned and looked at me with those giant blue eyes, and before she could reply, I said, "I love that you're a creative genius and that you don't bend your morals for anyone or anything. I respect you for that more than you can imagine."

I ordered the Chinese takeout, poured a couple of glasses of white wine, and sat down at the kitchen table beside Nancy.

"I guess I'm really striking out, huh?" she asked sadly.

"A few base hits and you'll be over three hundred in no time."

She swirled the wine in her glass.

"You keep that up and the wine is going to evaporate."

"It takes a very high temperature to vaporize alcohol."

"Thank you, Einstein," I joked then gently placed my hand over her hand holding the glass. "Don't you believe anything I tell you?"

"Of course I do. I wouldn't be here if I didn't."

The rest of the night was perfect. I got to watch two movies with my favorite actress, eat popcorn, drink a lot of wine, and hold the most beautiful girl in the world in my arms.

The next two weeks were more of the same and nearly as perfect, except for a few minor hiccups. Then came the day of reckoning, the day we were going to look at the new condominiums.

Nancy sat at my desk reading the newspaper; discarded sections were scattered on the floor around her. She had an excellent memory and had already used it against me many times, so I was confident that she hadn't forgotten today's planned activity.

It was easy for me to look past Nancy's many shortcomings. After all, I was in love with her. Her beauty blinded me; it impaired rational thought and sound judgment. I walked up behind her and kissed her neck, whispering, "We want to get to the open house early. Otherwise some of the better units might be gone."

She turned toward me and I could see the hurt on her face. "Yes, the condominiums. Wouldn't want to get there late."

She was still in her pajamas. Nancy! Pajamas! Condominiums! Movie dates! Popcorn and wine! It all seemed unreal, like a wonderful dream that turns into a nightmare, where you suddenly wake up to find yourself surrounded by the mundane: the domesticity of family, the smell of coffee and bacon, the chatter of familiar voices, and the distant sound of a radio broadcasting the news, weather, and sports.

Nancy dressed in an unusually sexy outfit and styled her hair very naturally. We decided to walk to the open house. It was less than half a mile and it was a typically beautiful southern California day. She talked about how much she enjoyed all the movies we had watched over the last couple of weeks, and said she was looking forward to the two movies she had planned for that night … two more Ingrid Bergman classics. She was disappointed that I didn't want her to cook dinner, but she was sure that would change. I didn't say much. It was better that way. I was already feeling a sense of guilt, like I was betraying the baby sister I never had or my long-dead mother.

We got to the building early, but the real-estate agent at the site kindly let us inspect the fourteen-unit complex on our own. She handed us a brochure that listed the dimensions and features of each unit. The association fee was a reasonable $110/month. The units were almost identical — all had two bedrooms, one and a half bathrooms, and a closed off balcony the size of a small closet. The architecture was California modern, which meant it lacked all style and was built cheaply. The major plus was the neighborhood; it was beautiful and retained a rustic and tranquil feel, a diminishing quality across much of the landscape of Los Angeles.

Nancy's reply to each unit we saw was either, "It's fine" or "It'll do." She sounded more like a frustrated, impertinent teenage girl than the energetic firecracker I knew. Finally, we reached a front unit that was slightly bigger than the others and much brighter and more airy. It had an open balcony, with an iron railing, that ran across the entire living-room area. It was nothing to jump with joy over, but compared to the apartment she had been living in two weeks before, it was like Heaven.

When I asked her how she liked it, she didn't even answer, just disappeared into the front bedroom, which looked out at the colonial-style First Christian Church across the street. I let her simmer for a while and then walked over to where she was standing at the window.

"What's wrong, Nancy?"

It took her a few moments to answer. "Is it because I'm Jewish that you don't want to marry me? If it is, I'll gladly convert to Catholicism."

I had to control myself so I wouldn't raise my voice. "Of all the insults you've thrown at me, that one hurts the most. Do you really think I'm the type of man who wouldn't marry a woman because of her religion?"

"The way I understand it, when Italian men get married, if the girl's not Italian, she better at least be Catholic."

"Is that the way you understand it? Using an ethnic stereotype to explain and dismiss an entire population?"

She looked like she might cry, and I almost thought she was playing me, but this was Nancy and she didn't lie. She was many things but not a fake, and she certainly wasn't like other women, at least not like any other woman I'd known. She turned and wiped tears from her eyes and said, "For the first time in my life, I came home to a house these last two weeks where I knew for certain that the man inside loved me."

"And I've felt the same way, Nancy. But we need to be sure about this. We have to be certain. I see so many crap marriages right here in LA. If we rush into marriage, we may end up regretting it, and I don't want either of us to feel trapped for the rest of our lives."

"What the hell do you mean, trapped? You just said you love me."

"Let me make this perfectly clear. I take marriage very seriously. I am not one of those people who swear before God to love someone forever and then change their mind two years later. All I'm saying, for both our sakes, is that I want to be absolutely sure, even more sure than I am now." I paused to see what she might say, but she was quiet. It seemed like she wanted to argue but knew she couldn't.

"How about this? Let's have a three-month trial. We'll live together for three months, and if everything goes as wonderfully as we expect, then we'll take the next big step. Is that okay?" I asked.

She threw her arms around me and held on tightly, as though she feared if she let go, this magical moment might forever dissipate.

"Do I at least get a ring?"

"A ring?"

"Yes! I want to show everyone that I'm taken. It doesn't have to be a big stone, just as long as it sparkles."

"Will my grandmother's ring that I have at the house do?"

"That would mean more to me than all the diamonds in the world."

We walked back to the house, and for the first time since meeting her, I could honestly see that Nancy was happy. It was as though the sun's rays were glowing within her body without any menacing clouds infringing upon her radiance. She was safe, loved, and finally free.

Back at the house, I opened the top drawer of my dresser and took out a box, placed it on the bed, and looked down at it for a long moment. In it were my most cherished belongings: letters my parents wrote when I was away at college; pictures of the three of us together celebrating birthdays and holidays; pictures of my parents as newlyweds; a copy of their will; the receipt and title that designates my burial plot next to theirs in Saint Raymond's Cemetery; my father's service medals and honors; and my grandmother's ring, wrapped in a silk napkin ... a simple, delicate ring signifying my grandparents' eternal love for each other.

I polished the ring with the napkin, and when I looked up, Nancy was standing a few feet away. I motioned for her to come closer and slid the ring on the third finger of her left hand. It fit perfectly.

Chapter Twenty-One

I drove down Sunset Boulevard toward Malibu. A month had passed since Maggie entered the rehab clinic, and she was being released. I had explained to Nancy in very clear terms that Maggie would always be part of my life, and if she tried in any way to interfere it would only cause problems. Nancy said she totally understood, looked admiringly at her engagement ring, and walked away.

I walked into Maggie's room and looked at her sitting on the bed. It was as if I was seeing her for the first time. She looked beautiful. Jumping up from the bed, she hugged me tightly. I could feel her exuberance pass directly into me like an infusion of oxygen.

When we got back to her house, her two children enthusiastically greeted her at the front door. She hugged and kissed them like only a loving mother could, and for the moment I felt relatively confident that my precious Maggie was back. Now more than ever she was my responsibility, and her children's welfare depended on her success, so I had to be vigilant and not let her down. Her recovery could unravel, and I was determined to support her so that wouldn't happen.

When I got home after seeing Maggie, I found Nancy sitting out at the pool just staring into space. She didn't move or even acknowledge my presence. This was not a good sign. I wondered if she was going to start in about Maggie. I tapped her on the shoulder, and as she turned she asked, "Can you please drive me to Sal's Mortuary in Glendale?"

Nancy's mother had died a few days earlier, and the mortuary had just called to tell her she could come down and pick up the ashes. She hadn't mentioned anything else to me; I was hesitant to start asking questions. We got into my car and drove to Glendale in total silence.

When we went into the mortuary, Nancy showed her identification, signed a number of papers, and was handed an urn with her mother's ashes. I tried to pay for the cremation, but Nancy in no uncertain terms said, "No!" She paid and we went back to the car.

The urn was ceramic and quite little. It looked more like an urn used to hold pet ashes. It was shaped like a baseball and Nancy was gripping it like a pitcher would, rotating the ball in her hand as if searching the seams for just the right feel. I asked, "So your mother was quite small?"

"No. I simply told them to pack her ashes tightly in the cheapest and smallest urn they had. Considering all the bitch did was eat junk food and watch TV, I would say they did a really good job."

Nancy had me park about a block away from a bridge overlooking the less-than-mighty Los Angeles River, directly across from CBS Studios, where The Mary Tyler Moore Show and its spinoffs were shot. We walked to the middle of the bridge, and, as I waited for Nancy to open the urn and release the ashes, it came to me that Nancy's mom had loved Mary Tyler Moore. It was a thoughtful, loving gesture on her daughter's part to spread her ashes so close to the place Ms. Moore had achieved entertainment magic and become famous. A moment later, Nancy threw the entire urn, like a baseball, off the bridge. It smashed into pieces against the cement bottom of the aqueduct and a small cloud of ash quickly dissipated ... that was it. No final words. Nothing.

She turned to me and said, "Now we are both officially orphans. At least your parents loved you."

"I love you, Nancy."

She smiled and took my hand. "I know, and that's all that matters."

We walked into the village to a Baskin-Robbins. Nancy ordered a double scoop of vanilla and I had a double scoop of chocolate-chocolate chip.

Chapter Twenty-Two

My nightmares started after I finished my first major campaign for a company marketing a vitamin supplement for teenage girls; the supplement promised to quickly cure acne. It was a major success for the two years it was on the market, which was one year more than the company ever hoped for. I didn't believe in the product, but then I wasn't being paid to believe, only to elevate the brand and increase revenue. My approach was no different than any major newspaper that ran advertisements for products their editorial staff knew were pure nonsense. A newspaper couldn't exist if its moral code was so uptight that it turned down advertising revenue from every company they didn't believe in.

To put it more accurately, it was one recurring nightmare. It always started with my coffin being rolled into Saint Raymond's Church in the Bronx, the church my parents and I had attended. I assumed I was in the coffin because where else would I have been?

The priest, a somber-looking man with the hardened complexion of a drunk, was shaking a canister of incense over my coffin while speaking in Latin. The church was empty except for a couple of professional mourners, old Italian women who always wore black. I doubted if any of them had cracked a smile in the last twenty-five years. Believe me, I was thankful that they were there. There's nothing worse than an empty funeral.

After the service was over, the coffin was placed in a hearse and driven to the cemetery by the lawyer who prepared both my parents' and eventually my own will. He was listening to The Beatles, which I thought was a nice touch because they are my favorite band of all time.

We passed through the gates of the cemetery and came to a stop just before my parents' graves, where the cemetery police met us. I was bewildered; I never knew the cemetery had its own police force. My lawyer, professional as always, handed the police captain the papers to the plot right beside my parents … my final resting place, as indicated in my carefully written will.

I could hear the police captain laughing hysterically, and to add insult to injury, I could hear my lawyer laughing right along with him. Apparently, another Joseph Rossetti — loving son of Stephen and Ann Rossetti — had just been buried in my plot a few days earlier.

Surely, there was some kind of major screwup. An imposter was buried alongside my parents! But my lawyer had another appointment — apparently with living clients — that he couldn't be late for. He dropped my casket off and drove off.

The police gathered around my coffin and started passing a flask of whiskey as they sang "La Marseillaise" in French. Suddenly Ingrid Bergman was beside me in the coffin, whispering, "Kiss me, Joe. Kiss me as if it were the last time." At that moment I didn't mind being dead or whatever the hell this was. Then, just as we were about to touch lips, *Poof!* she was gone, and all I could hear was torrential rain striking the casket.

The coffin started to move like a boat being steered by a drunken sailor. The streets were like one big gushing river. Traffic was stalled as the rising tide forced drivers and passengers to flee their cars. The only thing moving was my coffin, and in the distance was the Whitestone Bridge, like a beaming lighthouse in the midst of chaos.

The rain stopped but not before my coffin maneuvered its way beneath the bridge and into the East River. Floating, we passed the borough of Queens and then my coffin was in the middle of the Long Island Sound. I was alone, without anyone or anything in sight. I could feel the casket sinking, and, if being in the box of death wasn't claustrophobic enough, the sound of the swishing, swirling water made it nearly unbearable. I was thankful that at least my prick of a lawyer had followed my instructions and gotten the best watertight coffin on the market.

The descent went on forever. Never in my wildest of dreams would I have thought that the water in this part of the Sound was so deep. We drifted downward for what seemed like miles before hitting the bay floor. I was surrounded by trillions of tons of water, and, a moment later, water started to leak into the casket at an alarming rate! Apparently, my prick of a lawyer hadn't purchased a watertight coffin after all. Either that or they didn't have a casket on the market yet that could withstand that amount of pressure. I kicked and banged frantically in the enclosed space, but it was hopeless. My lips pressed against the coffin lid, my fate apparently sealed ... and it's then that I always woke up whistling "La Marseillaise."

And this nightmare had tripled in frequency since I met Nancy.

Chapter Twenty-Three

I arrived at work early. The lobby was empty except for the security guard, who was asleep behind the desk. Today was Maggie's first day back, and I wanted to make sure everything was perfect. I decided the less stress in her life, the less chance of a relapse. I ordered her flowers — even though I was sure she would have preferred jewelry — but I couldn't take a chance. I still hadn't told her about Nancy, and I didn't want her to get the wrong impression.

Even though more than a month had passed since her infamous last day at work, I couldn't purge myself of my overwhelming guilt over the part I'd played. When I got off the elevator, the first thing I heard was Jack's voice coming from his office. I was pretty sure he was now living there, mixing play and work, a true leader in every sense of the word.

I was inclined to walk straight to my office and hope he didn't see me, but his door was wide open. I decided it was better to just listen to whatever illogical advice he had to offer and get it over with. I knocked on the door, and to my surprise, Maggie was sitting across from him. She looked up at me with a slightly perplexed but amused smirk.

"I was just telling your beautiful assistant that the Japanese are getting anxious and want to start shooting the ad campaign as soon as possible, like today. Apparently, those rednecks have been protesting louder than ever about the foreign invasion into their holy territory."

"Tough selling fifteen dollars an hour when you're used to making a dollar-fifty an hour." I sat next to Maggie.

"Exactly, thank God for such ignorant fools. I need you and Maggie to drive up to Thousand Oaks. Maggie has the directions." Maggie waved the directions at me. "And the script with no dialogue."

We got up to leave and Jack held me back as he admiringly watched Maggie walk out his door toward our office. "Did she have some work done?"

"Not that I know of."

"Really, what a tight piece of ass. I can see now why you're so protective of her. And by the way, I got the two of you an extra-large trailer so you can do whatever it is that has our clients so in love with her."

I consulted with Maggie and she promised me that she was okay with the swiftness and unexpected nature of the project. It was exactly what she wanted: something new and exciting that would keep her on the straight and narrow. Besides, she had bills to pay and the extra money would come in handy. I reminded her that all her bills were taken care of.

"Exactly. Not only do I owe you my life, but roughly a million dollars."

"You owe me nothing at all except to promise you'll take care of yourself and never keep anything important from me again. And if you ever bring up owing me money again, I'll kick your ass."

She laughed as I walked into my office, picked up the phone, and called Nancy. I told her I would be gone from the office all day and when I told her where and with whom I was going, she screamed, "Fine!" and hung up on me. There is no word I despise more than that word, especially when a woman says it.

A few minutes later, Nancy called back. She apologized for the outburst and said it shouldn't be counted against her worthiness to be my wife. I should be pleased that she was jealous because it showed how much she was in love with me.

"Fine." I hung up quietly.

I decided against taking the company limousine, figuring driving ourselves would feel less awkward than sitting across from each other while trying to not talk about last month's events. I still wasn't sure what Maggie remembered, and I didn't want to upset her.

She looked up from the script she was reading. "Did you write this?"

"No, I just provided them with a general concept of what I thought needed to be in the commercial."

"Why does my character wear a crucifix around her neck?"

"The factory is being built in a part of Kentucky known as 'Bible Country.' The more we appease the fears of the general population that the Japanese have no intention of violating their cultural mores and beliefs, the less they'll protest."

She looked at me. "Can I borrow your crucifix?"

It was the first time in my life since my mother had given it to me that anyone had asked me to remove it, much less borrow it. Although my first impulse was to refuse, I couldn't say no, not at this difficult time. I was sure my mother would understand. The crucifix represented so much, not just the sacrifice Christ made, but also his teachings and a proper way to live our lives, how we as human beings should treat each other.

I pulled over to the side of the road. I removed the chain and crucifix and put it on Maggie. She looked down at the crucifix and lifted it to her mouth and kissed it, just like my mother used to do. At that moment, I was sure for the first time since she passed away that my mother approved of my actions.

Thousand Oaks was about an hour and a half from Los Angeles, but it may as well have been a thousand miles away. It had the feel of a small town; the streets were clean; there was no graffiti, and no rival gangs were fighting over turf. The homes and yards were large. Children rode bicycles up and down the streets, playing games, and there were even a few lemonade stands.

This wonderful atmosphere of peace and tranquility was helped significantly by the large number of LAPD officers who had moved their families to the area. Acutely aware of the dangers of the inner city, they were willing to spend four hours commuting each day. Thousand

Oaks was voted one of the safest cities in the United States year after year. Just outside the city limits there were green pastures with cows grazing and horses galloping. It wasn't Kentucky, but after the director, editor, and cameraman were finished, you would have a difficult time distinguishing it from Bluegrass Country.

The film crew was ready when we arrived. Maggie was ushered off to the makeup and wardrobe trailer. I walked around and talked briefly to the director and the crew, and off to the side I noticed four Japanese executives looking oddly out of place. I was pretty sure I recognized them from my presentation the month before.

They greeted me warmly and told me how excited they were that Maggie was going to star in the media campaign. But in a profession where weird was the norm, I still found their fascination with Maggie sort of unnerving. The executives all started clapping as Maggie came out of the trailer. Like her old self, she quickly responded to the applause, playing the part to perfection, bowing before each executive as they chanted, "Maggie! Maggie! Maggie!"

The director and the rest of the film crew looked on in amazement. When putting this campaign together, the idea that Maggie could so convincingly look the part of a Kentucky-born beauty — so pure and innocent — never even occurred to me, but apparently our clients saw something I never imagined. After a few mishaps in which the director yelled, "Cut!" and the executives booed, Maggie breezed effortlessly through filming; the director started calling her "One-Take Maggie."

The shoot was an amazing success. Maggie made three curtain calls after filming stopped and the executives kept chanting her name. In their eyes, a star was born, and to me it was a small but important step in her recovery. Maggie was aglow as we drove back to Los Angeles. "This is the first time I've felt beautiful in a long time."

I turned to look at her, but, as I was about to speak, she put her finger over my lips and said, "Remember our promise to each other. No lies ever again between us. It's time we start living up to that promise again."

It was late when I finally got home. I opened the door and followed the paper trail, picking up loose pieces of paper covered with incoherent notes, straight into the bedroom. Nancy was in bed reading a novel as I dropped the pile of papers on the bed next to her. "I was getting worried," she remarked.

"We hit a lot of traffic coming back."

"That's strange, you'd think all the traffic would be going the other way."

"This is Los Angeles. There's no reason or logic to our traffic woes."

She pulled back the sheet covering her body to reveal she was wearing red lingerie. If I didn't know better, I would have thought she was a model in a magazine — the epitome of sexy and beautiful. I was almost certain she could have turned a gay man straight, but at that moment I was exhausted and not in the mood for a critique of my performance.

"You look amazing, Nancy."

"It's all for you, Joe."

"That's really sweet, but I'm exhausted. I need to get some sleep."

I could sense her rage boiling as I took off my dress shirt and started to put on a T-shirt.

"Where's your crucifix?" she asked.

I touched my chest, and I realized that I hadn't gotten it back from Maggie.

"I let Maggie borrow it."

"Wow! That's an awfully personal item to lend to that ditzy little whore. Your mother must be turning over in her grave."

"You know something, Nancy? My grandmother is the one who must be spinning in her grave because she knows you're wearing her ring."

"That was uncalled for," Nancy replied as she got up from the bed and grabbed her book. "Totally uncalled for," she said once again as she walked out the room.

I lay on the bed feeling guilty even though she'd started it. I stayed there for around fifteen minutes and then walked into the living room where Nancy was lying on the couch reading her book. I sat down beside her, surprised that she hadn't taken the ring off.

"Nancy, please come back to bed."

"I'm fine right here. Besides, I'm no use to you in there since you're exhausted. Why not just go to sleep?"

"Why must you make everything so difficult, Nancy?"

"I'm sorry I'm a jealous bitch, Joe. Most guys would be flattered, but you're not like most guys, are you?"

"There's no reason to be jealous. Nothing is going on with Maggie."

"Don't you give me that shit! You're so protective of that little whore, I wouldn't be surprised if you were the father of her children."

I was boiling inside, but didn't have the energy to fight with her, so I simply asked, "What can I do to alleviate your stress?"

"You can marry me this week, instead of waiting two more months before making the obvious choice that any sane person in your position would make."

"You've got to be joking." I started to laugh. "At this moment in time, you are barely above the Mendoza line in my judgment."

"So in baseball lingo, I'm barely batting 200 … not anywhere good enough to be your wife?"

I was impressed. She was undeniably insane, but her knowledge and intelligence were astonishing. I shouldn't really have been surprised she would know about poor Mario Mendoza. He was an infielder whose career batting average over five years was so dismal that he came to represent an incompetence every other baseball player desperately tried not to emulate. Nancy loved statistics, and no other sport took so much pride in its statistics than baseball.

"Yeah, today was an awful day for you. It's like you played a doubleheader and you were 0 for 10. But then tomorrow you might actually get a few hits and raise your prospects."

"And what would you like me to do?"

"For starters, I don't want you anywhere near my bathroom. Just use your own bathroom from now on. Can you manage that?" I had started using the back bathroom. Sharing a bed with Nancy was heavenly; sharing a bathroom with her was hellish. In that skimpy red lingerie, looking into her big, blue eyes, all I could think was, *Yes, she's a lunatic, but she's my lunatic and I really don't want to share her with anyone.*

"How about we get married in two weeks?" she replied, as though we were negotiating.

"Didn't you hear a word I just said?"

"I heard it all; it's garbage and I don't believe any of it. By my own calculations, I'm batting way over 400. I'm the Ted Williams of prospective brides."

"Six weeks."

"Three weeks."

"One month and that's final." How did it get to this, negotiating with a psychotic genius? Easy, I was in love with her. Who else would come up with an atomic bomb genetically engineered to kill only the bad guys or a spray that castrates perverts? I don't care how many degrees she had from MIT and Stanford, any serious scientist would laugh at those ideas, or so I thought…

"A month! Four weeks! In essence, the month of February."

I agreed and we shook hands on it. "And we start from scratch, since your calculations are way off. Seriously, barely above the Mendoza line?"

I took her hand and we walked into the bedroom. She took off the lingerie and put on her favorite pair of pajamas and we went to sleep. Despite signing my life over to my lovely Nancy, I slept exceptionally well that night with no nightmares.

Nancy was already up when I walked into the kitchen the next morning. She was wearing a red bandanna to hold her hair back, and the first thing that went through my mind was how good that bandanna would look with the red lingerie.

She grabbed me by the hand and led me into her bathroom. I wasn't quite sure why she was showing it to me; it didn't look much different than the last time I'd looked inside, except that the bottles thrown randomly around were now placed on the bathroom counter, and the newspapers, notes, and books usually spread across the floor were shoved up against the tub.

"So, what do you think?" she asked excitedly. I didn't have the heart to tell her the truth, so I lied. "It looks great. I'm really proud of you."

She threw her arms around my neck and kissed me passionately. "You see? I can be perfect in so many ways."

Chapter Twenty-Four

Nancy didn't want a big wedding; she preferred a service at City Hall, or, if I insisted on getting married in a church, there was a little church on Coldwater Canyon that was at least non-denominational.

She couldn't commit to a honeymoon getaway right away but would make sure there was plenty of honeymoon activity in our bed or any other location in the house. She asked if I had any suggestions, and I replied only that she wear the red bandanna along with the red lingerie throughout the honeymoon period.

Jack called me into his office the second I got off the elevator. He closed the door and looked at me curiously as I sat down across from him. His office smelled of sex, booze, and cigars.

"I have a very important question to ask you."

"Sure, what is it? Surely no one complained about yesterday's shoot. Maggie was terrific. It went really well."

"No! No! They love that girl so much I wouldn't be surprised if they make her an honorary empress. I would like you to do me the honor of being my best man."

"What? You're getting married again? Are you joking? I thought you finally found happiness with the Russian whores."

"Yes, I have. But I didn't expect to fall in love with one." Jack took out the book and showed me her picture. "She's not only gorgeous; she's my soul mate. She understands my inner workings and accepts my overactive libido as a treasure of my manhood."

"What the hell does that even mean?"

"It means that she understands that no one woman could truly satisfy me or, for that matter, her. A rotation of them will be at our disposal at all times. They'll be like foster children with benefits."

"Living and sleeping in the same house with you?"

"Exactly! What better way to keep the excitement alive in a marriage? If only my ex-wives had been this forward thinking."

I wish I could say that I was stunned by this revelation. I knew it would be hopeless to even attempt to turn down his offer. The idea that I had been his best man for his last two failed marriages didn't seem to register. I accepted his offer, and to celebrate he poured us each a shot of Russian vodka, cheerfully exclaiming, "Glasnost! Glasnost!"

Maggie looked up from her desk and smiled. The entire outer office was filled with flower arrangements from her admirers.

"Feeling beautiful today?"

"Very much so, yes. And congratulations on being asked to be Jack's best man for a third consecutive time. It's quite an honor."

Chapter Twenty-Five

Nancy got into the car, leaned over, and kissed me long and passionately. "I've been waiting to do that all day."

She was in a talkative mood. "In exactly sixteen days I should start my period, unless of course there's some untold stress in my life that delays the onset." By this time in our relationship, nothing she said surprised me. In an unflattering comparison, she was Jack's female counterpart, except her IQ was way higher and she was drop-dead gorgeous. She continued, "So, by my calculations, the optimal point of my libidinous desires will be between twenty-three and twenty-six days from yesterday." She put dramatic stress on the word *yesterday*.

"While I'm not a traditional girl, I would like to get married on a Saturday. Twenty-eight days from yesterday is a Tuesday, so there's no way we can get married on that day. Luckily, I called the pastor at the church, and he assured me that he can marry us on the previous Saturday at ten o'clock in the morning. That's right during the time I'm going to be most hungry for sex."

I reminded her that the twenty-eight-day mark was not supposed to be the day we got married, but the day I'd decide if we were going to. Maybe six months down the road we'd actually do it.

She brushed my comment aside as though swatting away a fly. "Seriously, Joe, you're a smart guy. You think I'm going to wait another six months before getting married? I'm not a sex toy you can discard when you're ready for a new model. So, is that Saturday okay with you?"

"Yes, as long as you behave normally for the next three and a half weeks." I wasn't up to arguing with her, and I wasn't letting her go.

"I'm so happy we can work out these little problems so easily. We are going to have the most wonderful marriage."

She looked at my grandmother's ring on her finger for a long moment and asked, "I would really appreciate it if you would take back what you said last night about your grandmother and her ring."

"Okay, I take it back."

Nancy offered to cook dinner, which was an empty gesture considering we had nothing in the house to cook. We ordered pizza and then she went for a long swim. I sat by the pool and watched as she swam back and forth, thinking that never had I seen a more beautiful creature in or out of the water … and I was a big fan of both ducks and dolphins.

Nancy climbed out of the pool, grabbed a towel, and walked into the house. I followed closely behind as she left a trail of water from the living room straight into her bathroom. I tapped her on the shoulder just as she was about to close the door and pointed to the water on the floor. She apologized, threw me the towel, and asked if I could clean it up because she had to pee badly.

While in the bathroom, she also decided to take a shower. I sat on the couch, poured two glasses of wine, and watched as she walked into the living room dressed in her pajamas. She lifted her dry feet up for me to see and remarked, once again, about how perfect she was as she took a long drink from her glass. She reached over, kissed me enthusiastically, and said, "Oh, I can't wait for our honeymoon. We are going to have such a wild time. I promise." She finished the wine in her glass, walked into the bedroom, and went to sleep. I remained on the couch, thinking about the nothingness of it all.

That Nancy was so obsessively preoccupied with getting married was equally disturbing and flattering. She could have had anyone — movie moguls, famous actors, producers, directors, and heads of the largest companies in the world — but she decided she wanted me. Why? Seriously, why?

It couldn't be totally about money. Many bank accounts in this town would make me look like a pauper. Looks, no way. I might be described as easy on the eyes but I certainly was no Paul Newman or Robert Redford. Possibly my intellect and knowledge? I'm fairly sure I was the only guy in this town who shared her literary interests, but then she was into mathematics and physics, which I had virtually no interest in. Everything was a calculation, a mathematical certainty; she was a walking algorithm.

My pre-wedding gift to her was the purchase of a patent for a computer network she had designed; she had created the software and then built the system with a trusted team of MIT professors and former classmates. The money she could potentially earn from the patent — millions, if not billions, of dollars — didn't seem to concern her.

Nancy and I got married in the little church on Coldwater Canyon. Less than a half hour after the ceremony, she was dressed in the red lingerie and bandanna, as promised. We had been celibate for the three weeks prior to the wedding. I didn't bother with a prenup. In a liberal state like California it was useless; if Nancy ever did go to court to argue the prenup, she'd naturally win, and, instead of getting half my estate, she'd walk away with the entire thing. She was one persuasive little creature. No judge, male or female, would side with me.

She naturally had me sign a contract saying that I would never divorce her, and in turn she would never, ever grant me a divorce. In case of any infidelity on my part, she would not be responsible for her actions, but she promised that "the bitch would regret the day she was born," and after she was done with me she would never have to worry about me cheating on her again, but she would still never divorce me.

After making love, Nancy curled up next to me. She held me tightly, and it was then that I realized why she loved me. Like my father who protected my beautiful mother at all costs — so much so that he followed her to the grave — Nancy knew that I would protect her from all ghosts, past and present.

Chapter Twenty-Six

At first I was hesitant to tell Maggie about my marriage to Nancy, but then I realized that if I didn't tell her, the second I got to work she would be hearing it from my bride. I was quite sure that was Nancy's first official business of the day, telling her rival to back off. The battle was over and she was the uncontested champion.

Maggie took the news almost too wonderfully; my ego was sort of hurt. The male ego could be so fragile when women were involved.

She took off my crucifix, which she'd been wearing for the last month, and handed it to me. I gave her my credit card and told her to take an extended lunch break and buy one for herself. I would then go to church and have a priest bless it for her, like my mother had done for me. She still had a number of commercials to shoot, and each one required her to wear a crucifix.

I told her to be prepared for a call from Nancy, and, just as I opened my office door, the phone rang. And naturally, it was the happy bride.

We had matrimonial bliss for a while. I drove her to and from work, refusing to buy her a car. The roads were dangerous enough without her behind the wheel. I wasn't ready to become a widower because she couldn't pull herself away from an engrossing book she was reading while driving. She understood.

We ate at home every night except for the weekends. She offered to cook, but I insisted on takeout. After all, she worked as many hours as I did, and it wasn't fair for her to come home and have to cook. She understood.

She went for long swims every night after dinner, and I watched. I had to remind her every night after climbing out of the pool to dry the bottom of her feet and put on her slippers before going into the house. I told her I was only reminding her because I didn't want her to have to clean up the water she left behind on her way to the bathroom. She understood.

She took a shower, put on her pajamas, and curled up next to me on the couch. We drank wine and watched a movie. It was her turn to pick and she chose the films of Marcello Mastroianni. It was the best of all choices and, true to her word, we made love on the couch during the films, and afterward in bed, and in the morning before going to work. The idea that she was thinking about Marcello during our lovemaking didn't really bother me. I understood.

Once the Marcello marathon ended, Nancy reverted back to normal. The lovemaking was cut back to what one might expect from people married for twenty years, which at first didn't bother me. She was almost killing me with love, and I needed a rest. Nancy knew how to use her amazing body and good looks to her advantage, but sex itself seemed like an inconvenience to her ... except when Marcello was onscreen speaking in his native Italian.

We still continued to have dinner at home, but it became all seven days. After dinner she still went for a long swim, and I still reminded her to dry her feet and put on slippers before going into her bathroom. She would then change into her pajamas, sit on the couch with me for a short time, and drink a glass of wine. She would then disappear into her study for extended periods of time and wouldn't come to bed until I was about halfway through my recurring nightmare, which only made it worse because once I fell back to sleep, the nightmare didn't pick up from where it left off but started over from the beginning.

As part of Nancy's wedding gift I had given her the two back bedrooms so she could have some space of her own. One room she turned into her study, and after having them all sanitized by my two diligent housekeepers, her books, papers, and magazines were moved into her study, which I had lined with custom mahogany bookshelves. The ladies did a great job — literally turning dust and dirt into gold. In a matter of a few hours, it was like a tornado had ripped through the study, but Nancy was happy and nothing else mattered.

She turned the other room into her laboratory. That's where her computers, lab equipment, and blackboards were set up. I wasn't allowed into the laboratory for fear that I might accidently disturb or compromise the results of an important experiment. I had the same housekeepers cleaning my house once a week for twelve years but now needed them three times a week, and they were not allowed into Nancy's study or lab. I'm sure they considered that a blessing from God.

Married life continued to be wonderful, with no outrageous outbursts from Nancy. She seemed quite happy and content in her new home. She was the least materialistic woman I had ever met, and that's including my wonderful mother. She put her stamp on her two rooms and never once raised the subject of remodeling any part of house. She had no interest in jewelry other than her Star of David and my grandmother's ring. Her ears were pierced, but I never saw her wearing earrings. I guess when you're that beautiful and have a mind like Einstein, there's no need for extra adornments.

I sat back on the couch and turned on the news without any sound. The one anchor seemed kind of embarrassed. My first guess was that she had probably mispronounced Reykjavik, which was where Reagan and Gorbachev were having a summit meeting. I kind of felt sorry for her. I figured she hadn't been hired for her brains and was probably too busy before they went on the air with the makeup people to go over any hard-to-pronounce words.

A picture of a man's face covered in boils suddenly appeared onscreen and I turned on the sound. The camera then moved to the other anchor, who reported that three famous actors, their identities not yet released, had suddenly been stricken with a deadly virus that attacked their faces and genitals. After being taken to the emergency room at Saint Joseph's Hospital, where eyewitnesses reported them screaming in horrific pain, they were being kept isolated at the hospital and under close guard.

An unidentified nurse told a reporter that one of the men tried to urinate, but the pain was so excruciating that he passed out on the bathroom floor. Since then, all three men were fitted with catheters and placed under heavy sedation. The numerous boils on their faces and genitals were said to be as big as half-dollars.

The camera switched back to the first anchor, who said that they would keep abreast of this breaking story but for now it was time for sports. "And how did our Dodgers do tonight?" she asked the sports anchor as she regained her composure and flashed a winning smile. After finding out the Yankees' score, I shut off the TV and went to bed.

Chapter Twenty-Seven

I dropped Nancy at work and went straight to the office. Maggie was intently reading the newspaper at her desk. I asked what was so interesting and she replied, "Didn't you hear about the three actors and the mysterious virus? Some tabloids are reporting that now they're on life support. Boils the size of baseballs on their dicks and faces. It couldn't have happened to three more despicable lowlifes."

"Why would you say that?"

"The girls I know at the studio have been complaining about these three pieces of shit for years. Groping, harassing, in a few cases actually raping a few young actresses and crew members. The executives have always turned a blind eye to the accusations and complaints. Your wife must know these guys. I wouldn't be surprised if she does their makeup."

"I'll have to ask her." I felt my blood pressure rising and my heart racing. I walked into my office and sat down at the desk. I inhaled and exhaled a few times as I looked down at the phone. Nancy was vindictive, but she had morals. Sure, she cut off her father's dick, but the son of a bitch deserved it. You would have thought cutting off the bastard's dick was enough, but to let the pervert bleed to death seemed a little much. I had to find out if she was responsible for the boils. Nancy answered when I called. She was so happy to hear from me that I couldn't get up the nerve to ask her the question.

Maggie walked into my office with a can of Lysol and said, "Either you do something or I'm calling the health department. The smell coming out of Jack's office is gross, and everyone's scared that the source of the boil epidemic might be our fearless leader and the company he's keeping."

I took the bottle, knocked on Jack's door, and handed it to him. I looked at his face carefully but didn't see any boils. "The staff is seriously threatening to call the health department, Jack. I would strongly advise sanitizing this place." He nodded, closed the door, and I walked back to my office and flopped down on the couch.

The outbreak was all over the news. All programs were being interrupted with updates on the condition of the three actors. The boils were growing. According to unidentified sources, they were now the size of softballs. A tabloid had somehow obtained pictures of the men's genitals and published an early edition with the caption TAKE COVER. Medical specialists, especially dermatologists, were being interviewed, and they all agreed it was most likely a virus transmitted through intimate contact. Boils were highly contagious, and even a miniature fissure in any of the boils could spread the venom like radiation.

A few specialists even postulated that this might be an offshoot of the HIV/AIDS virus. They showed pictures of men in Kenya with similar boils all over their bodies as proof that this was very likely AIDS-related. The three affected actors were allegedly "closet homosexuals" according to unidentified sources, colleagues, friends, and family.

Prominent religious leaders throughout the country warned that this was God's retribution against the unholy and immoral ways of Hollywood. "Abstinence is the only defense against this plague."

Pictures of doctors and scientists in hazmat suits treating the men were appearing everywhere. Politicians wearing surgical masks tried to tell the population to be calm. Reports of more men affected by the virus being taken to hospital were being reported throughout the city. The residents of West Hollywood, the first recognized gay city in the United States, were told not to travel outside the city limits. Police barricades were being set up to ensure that no one could leave.

Psychics and doomsayers predicted that the virus would eventually affect the entire human race and that the cosmic energy would be so great that all the boils would burst simultaneously, drowning all of humanity in a gigantic cesspool of pus.

I called Nancy again and told her that she needed to leave work immediately since her studio was where the first three victims had last been seen before the outbreak. She told me to relax and said that people were overreacting. She was so calm that it only heightened my suspicion that she was somehow implicated in this virus. When I picked her up after work, she greeted me with a big kiss. I couldn't help noticing that the studio lot looked nearly empty. "So did any of the people you work with evacuate early?"

"Oh, they all did," she replied nonchalantly.

I didn't want to admit it, but I couldn't help thinking: *Was Nancy actually a cold-blooded killer?* I just didn't have any concrete proof. When we entered the house, I steered her into a walk-in closet next to my bathroom and closed the door. I couldn't wait another second. I had to ask her.

"Nancy, I love you. Now tell me the truth. Are you at all responsible for this virus?"

"Yes," she said, as coolly as if I had asked if she wanted a glass of wine.

"You're joking, right? Please tell me you're joking."

"No, Joe. For the thousandth time, I never lie."

"Couldn't you lie just once, Nancy? Just once, in the name of love?"

"No!"

"Did you have any accomplices?"

"No."

"Just tell me, why?"

"Because they're disgusting pigs. Groping, harassing, even raping a couple of young actresses and threatening them that if they told anyone, they would never work in this town again."

"Why not file a complaint with Human Resources or with upper management?"

"I did, along with numerous other women, but nothing ever came of it. Don't be so worried; in about two hours, they'll start to miraculously recover. Their immune systems will bounce back and the boils will disappear. Except for temporary paralysis to their genitals, they'll be fine, and for a time the women of the world will be safe."

"So instead of being charged with three counts of murder in the first degree, you're only going to be charged with three counts of attempted murder? That definitely makes me feel better."

"I'm not going to be charged with anything. They'll never be able to trace it back to me. I've covered my trail perfectly."

"Nancy, you leave a trail walking from the living room to the bedroom. Do you actually believe for one moment that the authorities aren't already on to you?"

"They think it's some type of airborne virus or a communal virus like AIDS or syphilis. What I engineered is pure brilliance: my virus blocks the flow of red blood cells to targeted parts of the human anatomy, and then, just as those cells are about to expire, the release of life-saving cells and an ample supply of oxygen keeps those sick perverts alive, but their dicks are temporarily paralyzed."

"Are you insane?"

"I'll pretend you didn't ask that."

"Go get your passport. We need to leave the country. I'll have a private plane waiting for us at the airport in less than an hour."

"Sorry, Joe, but I can't leave. I'm too close to my greatest achievement ever, and it's all because of you. You were right; I can't create an atomic bomb that discriminates between good guys and bad guys, but I can create a conventional bomb with a radius of two miles, with specific genetic coding that can, with an 80 percent probability, kill the bad guys with limited civilian causalities. I promise we can go on a long vacation once I'm finished."

I looked at her, dumbfounded, hoping that this was just an add-on to my recurring nightmare. How could she be so beautiful and intelligent while also being so friggin' deranged?

"I've already spoken with scientists in Israel, Britain, and here in the United States about my breakthrough. They are all greatly impressed."

"And exactly when did you get in touch with them?"

"Just recently, in the last few days." She kissed me on the cheek. "Not a thing to worry about, my wonderful, adorable husband."

A few seconds later, I heard loud banging on the front door and police helicopters circling above the house. I opened the door and was handed two search warrants: one from the police and one from the FBI. Less than a minute later, Nancy and I were handcuffed and read our rights. I didn't even bother to remind her to keep her mouth shut and not answer any questions. That would have been a waste of time.

Chapter Twenty-Eight

I was released on half-a-million-dollars bail. Nancy was denied bail as the prosecution claimed she posed a real threat to national security. It was painful to watch the court officers escort her back to jail. Since getting back home, we hadn't spoken, but her lawyer, a high-powered Los Angeles attorney and friend, was confident that she'd eventually be exonerated, if that was what I truly wanted...

I took a beer out of the refrigerator and drank it quickly as I walked through the living room. I opened the sliding door, walked outside, and sat beside the pool. After a few days behind bars, I felt like a different man. Suddenly I appreciated all the things I had taken for granted, such as closing the bathroom door, eating food that actually had taste, and falling asleep in the quiet of my own house without hearing the other inmates.

After about ten beers, while I sat counting the ripples across the pool, my lawyer called. He told me that after further review, the prosecution had dropped all the charges against me. The military said the charges of treason and sedition were absurd, and the government played dumb. My bail money was already being transferred back into my account. I was relieved but not greatly surprised. I was a friend to the military and had recently put together an uplifting and patriotic ad campaign. Recruitment and enlistment were way up, which was especially impressive after all the negative coverage after Vietnam. "Morning in America" was real, at least to those young recruits listening to President Reagan's masterful ability to communicate. I had also put together a winning campaign for the LAPD, which highlighted their very special and dangerous job protecting the citizens of our great city. Personally, I think I was helped by divine intervention, because there were so many negatives to deal with that even I was shocked by its success.

I asked about Nancy, and the lawyer said he had seen her earlier, but she was extremely difficult and threatening to defend herself. I told him not to argue with her and act as though he agreed with her. "She has a way of wiggling out of the worst messes. I bet she already has you obsessing about how wonderful it would be to have sex with her." A very long pause on the other end confirmed I was right.

I was asleep when the phone rang. It was three o'clock in the morning, Nancy's favorite time to call. She was ranting and terribly upset that I hadn't come to visit her when I was released. I tried to explain that I had had enough of jail after spending two days behind bars. I needed a day off, but I promised I would definitely be there tomorrow. I told her that all the charges against me had been dropped, which sent her into another insane rant about why I was sleeping and horsing around instead of working on a way to get her free. I reminded her that she had been denied bail and there was nothing I could do. She laughed crazily and screamed, "Don't you give me that, you son of a bitch! You're more connected than the President of the United States."

"That may be so, sweetheart, but in this case everyone is running for cover. Espionage and treason are serious crimes. You should have thought about that before making contact with foreign governments and trying to sell them weapons of mass destruction."

"Oh, give me a break. The only governments I had contact with were friends of the United States. I'm the most patriotic person in this whole country."

"Okay, well, next time you see the judge, don't forget to mention that. I'm sure he'll feel the same pain for you that I do."

"That's not funny."

"I got you the best lawyer in town. You're in good hands."

"The only thing that son of a bitch is interested in is fucking me. Your wife!"

That was true, but I didn't give her the satisfaction of agreeing with her. "Give the man a chance. He's worked miracles for clients nearly as deranged as you."

"Get me the hell out of here, Joe," she started to cry. "I can't last here much longer."

"Don't worry about it, doll. I'll start working on it first thing tomorrow morning, but I wouldn't get your hopes up. You be careful in there. I'm sure your fellow inmates haven't seen a piece of ass like yours in a long time. Probably never! I love you, Nancy."

She hung up the phone without a reply and I went back to sleep.

The following morning I woke up again to the beautiful California sunshine pouring in my bedroom window. I felt rejuvenated. I got up, made myself some coffee, picked up the *Los Angeles Times* from my lawn, and saw the front-page picture of my wife being escorted out of the courtroom, handcuffed, back to jail. Even in jail attire and wearing no makeup, she was still the most beautiful thing I had ever seen. I skipped the article about Nancy and went straight to the sports section.

I called work and told Maggie I was taking the rest of the week off. She had seen the news and asked me fifty questions in twenty seconds, clearly concerned and upset. I assured her that I was safe and everything would turn out okay.

Jack asked if I could review some ad proposals we had just received from a major corporation that insisted I be in charge. It was worth millions to the company and a large percentage would come to me. Of course I said yes. Who was I to get in the way of making money? Especially now that I had Nancy's legal defense to pay for, the bonus would be welcome.

The lawyer called shortly after that and told me he was going to see Nancy. He asked if I wanted to come along, but who was I to get in the way of a budding romance? The poor guy had it bad.

It was eerie that I could smell Nancy's perfume all over the house. I summoned the courage to open the door to her study and found it an absolute disaster — papers piled high, books flung randomly across the room, and unrecognizable formulas scribbled on the chalkboards. Most of the action had taken place here when the FBI and local police entered with their search warrants. I must admit, though, it didn't look any worse than before the intense search. If anything, it seemed as though law enforcement might have tidied up the place.

Work sent over the new project, an ad campaign for a new drug that dramatically relieved the effects of severe depression. The FDA had just given it final approval following extensive clinical trials. All the test results had come back favorable and with limited side effects. Pharmaceutical companies were incredible; they had no problem throwing tens of millions of dollars into advertising campaigns. Despite the costs of research and advertising, for every dollar spent bringing a drug to market the company made ten, at least for the first seven years in which it exclusively held the patent. They could cry wolf all they wanted before an endless stream of congressional committees, but many of these companies were as big as IBM, US Steel, and Apple.

I arrived at the prison a half hour before visiting time was over. I sat down in a chair facing a glass partition that separated visitors from prisoners, the same setup you see in the movies. Nancy, wearing an orange jumpsuit, was escorted to the chair opposite me. She picked up the phone on her side just as I picked up mine.

"Hi Nancy, how are you doing? Let me tell you, you look hot in prison garb. Are you wearing panties and a bra under that outfit?"

"Fuck you!" she replied as she held the telephone in one hand and twirled her hair with the other. I held up the front page of the newspaper so she could see her picture.

"I thought you might like to see this. I was thinking I'd frame it and hang it beside our bed to remind me to come visit you occasionally over the next twenty-five years."

"Funny! What are you doing to get me out of here?"

"Not much I can do, sweetheart. Espionage and treason are serious crimes; they have a shitload of incriminating evidence against you."

"Don't you give me that shit! You're walking around free."

"That's because I'm not guilty of anything."

"I'm your wife!"

"I'm aware of that, and it's a real shame that we're going to have to spend so much time apart over the next couple of decades."

"You motherfucker!"

"Now, now, Nancy. I know it's important to pick up the prison lingo to survive, but it doesn't do you any good to use that language around me. You know how much I hate a foul mouth on a woman."

"You're enjoying this, aren't you? You piece of shit!"

I took out my house keys and held them up to the glass partition.

"Keys, Nancy. Keys lock and unlock doors. Right now, you're guaranteeing that these keys of yours will never again unlock any door. In fact, I just might lose them."

She called the guard to take her back to her cell, turning one last time to give me the finger. Such a peach!

When I returned home and opened the front door, naturally the first thing I smelled was her. She was inside my head, occupying all my senses, and wreaking havoc on my ability to distinguish between reality and fantasy. I went to the liquor cabinet and poured myself a double of Jack Daniels. I shot it down and immediately felt better. Everything became much clearer. She was my wife and I loved her immensely. "For better or worse" was part of the wedding vows, and I wasn't the type of guy who went back on his word.

The upside was surely that it couldn't get any worse. The downside was that even if I managed to arrange for a more lenient judge, it might cost me at least a million dollars in bail, and it would be just my luck that the spaceship that dropped her off on Earth would return to pick her up, which would mean a lot of wasted money. I poured myself another double and shot it down, then grabbed a beer from the fridge, turned on Frank Sinatra, and walked out to the pool.

I took off my shoes, sat down on a beach chair, and marveled at Sinatra's voice. At times it seemed he was speaking directly to me. I don't know if I'd had this connection with him before or only since meeting Nancy. My guess was that it started after she turned my world upside down.

My parents would probably have loved Nancy — at first. When she tried, she made a wonderful first impression. Her astonishing beauty gave her an immediate advantage, and my mother would have quickly started preparing for the arrival of her grandchildren. Once they had arrived — and they finally acknowledged the painful truth that their daughter-in-law was off the wall — they most likely would have kidnapped our children, moved to a foreign country like Florida, and raised them correctly with an abundance of love and compassion. It would have been all for the best.

I stood up and walked back into the house to review the proposal for the new drug; suddenly I remembered a picture I kept in my desk at Stony Brook. It was of this beautiful girl with long, shiny dark hair and large brown eyes looking out a window. She was my age, but the look in her eyes was of deep sorrow, unbearable melancholy, and the lost promise of any happiness. I used to think that if I could only meet her, talk with her, and get to know why she was unhappy, maybe I could bring sunshine and promise back to her life. I never knew why, but I was sure of it.

That picture haunted me throughout my entire time at Stony Brook. At times I saw the same haunted look in Nancy's eyes, but I couldn't say I believed for sure that I could ease her pain. I couldn't say with any certainty that I could ever fully understand her, but her stunning beauty and intelligence had won me over. She was my wife; I loved her, and I felt responsible for her safety.

I wrote down a few notes about the girl in the picture, her downcast eyes against a dark and depressing background. Slowly, her eyes looked up as rays of sunshine cut across her face, an engaging smile emerged as the sound of laughter and festive music rang out magically across a scenic garden of waterfalls, children playing, and dogs chasing balls across open fields. The girl took the hand of a young man. The fog of depression gone, an illuminating clarity and purpose took hold as they looked into each other's eyes and kissed. Life reinvented! Life renewed! Rebirth and promise!

I opened another beer, closed the sliding door, and looked out onto the pool. Ten years ago, I never would have imagined moving to Los Angeles. Then my mother unexpectedly died and before her tombstone was placed, my father died. They had just finished paying off their little palace in the Bronx. By even the most pessimistic measures, they should have lived at least another twenty years. For days, I stared at insurance policies and bank accounts worth nearly half a million dollars. I cashed everything in, sold the house, and put it all into an account I named "Mom and Dad." And I've never taken a penny out of it.

Before relocating to Los Angeles, I bought a plot in Saint Raymond's Cemetery next to my parents. In my will, I clearly stated that when I died, my body was to be sent back to the Bronx and buried there. Before I realized the full truth about my wife, I had made her the executor of my will. Considering her altered state of mind, that would have to change; she might use my body for research and toss the remains in the garbage.

I had a few more beers and called it a night. I didn't bother setting the alarm clock because I didn't have to go to work and hadn't decided when I was going to put the pressure on to get my wife released … certainly not before noon. Naturally, just after I fell into a deep sleep, the phone rang. I picked it up, dazed and confused. "Yes, Nancy?"

"You sound terrible. Is someone else there?"

I didn't bother justifying the question with a reply. "What do you want?"

"I want to make up. I'm willing to forgive everything you've done."

"I haven't done anything."

"Exactly. While I've been rotting here in jail, you've been sitting on your ass, getting drunk."

"Goodnight, Nancy. I love you."

"Don't you dare hang up that phone. After you left this afternoon, I got a visit from the FBI and the DOD."

"The Department of Defense?"

"Yes, and they offered me a job. They looked over my research and they're highly impressed."

"Is this some type of joke?"

"No, you jackass. They recognize genius when they see it."

"So when are you getting released?"

"That's the problem. The FBI is willing to drop all the charges, but the local authorities are being dicks and won't go along with it. They still want to charge me with intent to inflict bodily harm on those perverts, even though they're now totally fine and back to work. It's time you put some pressure on your friends. The FBI and military will drop all charges once they're guaranteed that the state prosecutor won't pursue the case. They have to drop all those inane charges."

"Okay," I said meekly.

"Okay? What the hell does that mean?"

"It means I'll do everything I can. Do you really expect me to start making phone calls now?"

"Yes, that is exactly what I expect you to do."

"Love you, Nancy. Bye." I hung up the phone and blocked incoming calls.

Only a few minutes before I had been sound asleep, but I couldn't get back to sleep if someone shot me with an elephant tranquilizer. I went to the refrigerator and did the only thing I could do under such stressful circumstances — I had a beer and then another and another.

By the time it started getting light outside, I was getting antsy. I picked up the phone and called Nancy's lawyer. I could hear his wife in the background asking who was calling so early. He assured her it was just a client. I told him everything Nancy had said, and then I had to tell him again because he was in a fog. I told him the best course of action was to threaten the perverts and studio heads with front-page stories of rape and sexual harassment. That would make them rethink the charges they had filed against Nancy. He loved the idea and hung up the phone.

Hours — and many beers — later, I got a call from the lawyer. The actors and studio heads shit their pants when he threatened to go public with the accusations. Smelling blood and good old-fashioned cash, he told them that his client's career was over because of the actions of these sexual predators. He would take nothing less than two million dollars in compensation. They countered with a million and settled on a million and a half. All charges against Nancy, federal and state, were dismissed. She called me as they were processing her release paperwork and said she'd regained her faith in me. I decided the best course of action was not to reply and hung up. Then I took a shower, rinsed my mouth a half a dozen times, and called a limousine to pick me up.

I sat at the very back of the stretch limo. Privacy was of the utmost importance when talking to Nancy since her ideas could be quite disturbing. The less people heard, the less chance of her being re-arrested. I had the driver pull over at a liquor store. I picked up two bottles of Cristal and stuck them in an ice bucket provided by the service. We arrived early at the prison. I stayed in the car and talked to the driver about sports until I spotted Nancy coming out with the lawyer. She was dressed in the clothes they had taken her away in. Strangely, I had imagined, or more to the point, hoped, she would still be wearing the orange jumpsuit. I was disappointed.

I told the driver to wait in the car as I got out and greeted my lovely wife and her suitor. We talked for a while and then the lawyer went his own way. Nancy commented, "That pig freaks me out. I could feel his eyes on every part of my body."

I opened the door to the limo and Nancy slid in. "Thank you, sir." I slid in beside her and closed the door.

"That pig negotiated a generous compensation package for you with your former employer."

"I know. He wouldn't stop mentioning it as though he was expecting a little something extra on top of his thirty-three percent fee."

"A million dollars in the bank and a new and exciting job. Not bad compensation for a few days behind bars."

She looked at me and smiled. "Just like you to put a positive spin on an injustice and a fabrication of the truth. I think I'll give that money to charity."

"Not so quick, Nancy. That money will pay legal fees and other expenses I incurred because of you."

"Whatever! Do as you please. Dirty money and you go together like a horse and carriage."

"Cute."

"I've had a lot of time to think while you fiddled around like an absent-minded adolescent."

"It's not like you served thirty years. You were in jail for four days."

"Two more than you."

"Wow! Are we actually comparing jail time?"

"No, that would be silly, but it is a problem. I'm on a much higher plane than you."

"Yet you needed me to get you out of jail."

"I didn't say you were useless. If that were the case, I wouldn't be married to you and I certainly wouldn't love you as much as I do. I can honestly admit that you are the only man I have truly loved unconditionally."

"Thank you, Nancy. That's very sweet."

"I don't expect a reciprocal response from you. After all, you had lovely and compassionate parents, and I would never come between that bond."

She folded her legs and looked curiously down at the bottles of champagne. Like always, I was left to figure out the riddle. I picked up a bottle, removed the cork, and poured us two glasses. I handed her a glass and smiled. I still had the image of her alive and kicking in that orange jumpsuit. Strange, because orange was my least favorite color, but Nancy was always my preferred dish. We raised our glasses and I made a simple toast. "To freedom!" Nancy quickly finished her champagne, and I refilled her glass. "Thank you, sir."

She looked at me and smiled deviously. "I don't want to ruin the moment, but I'm bleeding profusely down there." She pointed between her legs. "Strange, it started just about the time you hung up on me this morning."

"That's playing dirty."

She laughed as she polished off her second glass of champagne. She moved closer, ran her hands through my hair, and kissed me passionately. All else went dark after that.

Chapter Twenty-Nine

After picking up my lovely bride from jail, drinking champagne in the limo, and making out like two teenagers, I had the chauffeur drive us up the coast. I figured it was best not to go home yet with some news crews still hanging around the house. The city prosecutor had hastily called a news conference and explained that there wasn't enough evidence to prosecute and that the supposed victims were just happy to get on with their lives. So there wasn't much of a story left, but that didn't stop the press from pursuing it. The last thing I needed was Nancy unwisely answering some stupid question on her way to the front door.

I asked Nancy if she knew what the government was going to have her working on. She whispered that she wasn't allowed to tell me because that might put my life in *danger*, and she wouldn't know what to do if anything, God forbid, happened to me. The way I saw it, if the government was insane enough to hire her, let them handle the fallout when she went rogue.

We got back late and found no news crews at the house. Nancy immediately went to her laboratory; I could hear her gasp when she noticed the missing computers.

"Did they say if they were going to bring them back?"

"I didn't even ask. I was too busy getting you released to give it much thought. I would just let them go. After all, now you're going to be working with advanced military software and computers much better suited to your intellect."

"And what do you think my computers were designed to handle?"

I walked away and she grabbed me by my shoulder. "Can you buy me new computers?"

"No!"

"How about all the money you said the studio gave me as compensation?"

"Legal bills."

"Nonsense!"

I turned to look at her sad, pleading face. "You'll never see a penny of that money, so I recommend that you get your daily fix of computers and software at your new job."

"You son of a bitch!"

"Now, now, my beautiful little bride, is that any way to talk? How about we go shopping tomorrow for a diamond necklace or a closet full of Armani jackets perfectly tailored to your wonderful dimensions? Then we can stop off at a bookstore and buy you as many literary classics as you like. How does that sound?"

"Why don't you go screw yourself?"

"I would, but, as you know, it's anatomically impossible."

"Not after I get through with you."

I laughed as I walked to the kitchen to get myself a beer. She yelled, "Why do you have to be so mean?"

"Because that might be the only way to keep you out of jail. I love you so much, Nancy. Even if we never sleep together again, knowing you are here, safe in our home, is better than having to come visit you in jail for the next thirty years."

She hugged me and kissed me passionately. It was a small victory, but when it came to Nancy, any victory was a reason to celebrate.

The following morning, I opened the front door to a young military officer holding a parcel of documents the Department of Defense had sent over for Nancy. He wouldn't let me sign, nor would he accept my invitation to come into the house. Nancy, dressed in her bathing suit and dripping wet, signed for the parcel after showing the officer her ID. She placed the parcel on the living-room table and went back out to the pool to finish her swim, leaving a trail of water behind. I opened the parcel and took out the documents. I had dealt with the military before and wasn't about to have Nancy signing over her rights and freedoms just to get herself in front of a computer.

The first few pages were standard forms, not much different than the forms I had signed when I did a number of ad campaigns for the military a few years back. Sworn statements saying that while working for the DOD you wouldn't disseminate any information, top secret or not, to any foreign country, corporations, or individuals in or outside the DOD. Such violations would constitute treason and the perpetrator(s) would be tried before a military tribunal.

The following pages dealt with the issue of patents and stated that any prior patent (relevant to the agreed-upon work as stated above) was to be purchased by the US government at a market value consistent with other military purchases. The five patents that I had registered with the patent office on Nancy's behalf were listed and the DOD was offering $50,000 for each one. All other work, whether started or completed while in the service of the DOD, was property of the United States.

I turned to the last page of the document and to my delight saw that it came from the office of General Pierce, a friend who had assisted me on the military ads. I called his personal number. He picked up immediately, and, from all indications, he'd been expecting my call. He reminded me that the documents were for my wife's eyes only, and if she needed any clarification a military lawyer would be assigned to help her. He then started to laugh as I brought up the meager sum his department was offering for her valuable formulas and software, which would greatly enhance the security of the United States.

He laughed again. "Don't forget that your wife was facing treason charges just two days ago and possibly a date with the electric chair. That alone should make her agree to our terms."

Dripping wet, Nancy sat down on the couch and angrily grabbed all the papers out of my hand. She was just about to open her big mouth when I put my hand over it.

"Now, General, you and I both know that Nancy never intended to hurt our country. She's the most patriotic person I know."

"Another Hedy Lamarr," the general remarked, "and if you don't mind me saying so, just as beautiful. Are you aware of how much Ms. Lamarr was paid for her patented invention, which helped us defeat the Nazis? Very little, Joe."

"Well, we wouldn't want to make that mistake twice, would we?"

"No, we wouldn't. I'll tell you what, why don't you ask for ten times the amount we offered and I'll see what I can do. Please give your brilliant wife my regards, and tell her to report to work in a week."

The general hung up, and I said to Nancy, "The general sends his best."

Chapter Thirty

The general came through and Nancy received ten times the original offer, which immediately told me that her software was extremely important to the military and the security of the United States. When I told her about the $2.5-million payment, she simply remarked, "What good does it do me? It's not like you'll let me buy what I want."

"Apparently, your invention is a huge deal, so the military is willing to pay top dollar even though they could have convicted you for treason and legally confiscated the software for nothing."

"That would've given them the answer to only half the riddle. The other half is up here," she pointed to her head. "For the record, I would have given them the rights to the patents for nothing. I'm a patriot."

"Of course you would have." I took her into my arms. "Either way, I am amazingly proud of you. Is it okay if I say so?"

"Of course."

"And I love you very, very much."

"And how do you plan on proving that?" I kissed her again.

Nancy's association with the DOD was troubling because it didn't take a genius to realize she was unstable. It didn't alleviate my anxiety that every morning she was picked up for work by two muscular, well-armed agents in a bulletproof black SUV and then dropped off each night by two different agents, also muscular and well-armed. She was a top priority, and I was certain it had nothing to do with her looks.

Her workdays grew steadily longer, and eventually she only had

Sundays off. It got to the point that the only time I saw Nancy, besides Sundays, was early in the morning and then late at night when she would quietly slip into our bed, cuddle up next to me, and hold me increasingly tighter and tighter throughout the night.

She insisted that she loved the work she was doing, but she couldn't tell me anything else because it could jeopardize my life. I kept both our passports close by at all times.

Chapter Thirty-One

During my much-needed vacation after the stint in jail and then ensuring Nancy's release, I kept in constant contact with Maggie. I normally would have told her to take the week off, but an idle mind is a dangerous thing, and an idle mind for an addict is playing with fire. I kept her busy at work, probably with more projects than I had given her in the last seven years. I was pretty sure she knew why, but she didn't complain.

I asked George, our limousine driver, to keep a close watch on Maggie while she was at work and then follow her home. He was secretly in love with her but he wasn't her type — rich — so he never asked her out; he was also a key source of information on our fearless leader, Jack. I knew George had the pleasure of driving Jack and his entourage around into the wee hours of the morning and probably took notes, which he handed to Maggie the second she walked through the door in the morning.

When I got off the elevator at work, I was greeted by a chorus of fellow employees giggling and singing, "Hi, Joe." Finally, I made it over to Maggie's desk that was adorned, as always, with floral arrangements from her Japanese admirers. She was carefully selecting boxes in a pool that was going around the office.

"Hi, Joe." No giggling.

"Can I get in?"

"Of course you can. It's $20 a box. How many would you like?"

"Five."

"Great! I'll save them for you. That way no one can say it's rigged."

I was puzzled, but before I could say another word, she explained. "There are thirty boxes representing thirty calendar days. The day your wife makes you her next victim and your body is covered with boils — let's say in ten days — the person with box number ten is the winner."

I opened my wallet and handed her $100. "All the charges against Nancy were dropped, you know."

"Of course. And remember our promise never to lie to each other?"

I looked at her, my precious Maggie, and for a moment it all seemed normal again. "You're right. My wife was guilty as sin."

Maggie followed me into the office. "I'm going to get a cappuccino. Would you like one?"

"No, thank you." I sat in my chair and looked at her.

"How are the children doing?"

"You know, that's the sixty-third time in a little over a week you've asked about my kids. The last time I checked, they should be graduating college soon."

"Don't be such a wiseass."

She laughed and turned away. I continued to watch her as she walked toward the elevator. Just a few months ago, I would have thought Maggie was the last woman in the world some guy would take advantage of, and yet it had happened. I knew that she could start using again at any time and I couldn't keep watch over her twenty-four hours a day. If I hadn't met Nancy and fallen for her, I would have simply married Maggie. That would have given me a measure of control over her that I would have felt comfortable with ... even though after her second marriage, I'd given up the idea of ever marrying her.

The only good thing that came out of Nancy's incarceration was that, for a short time, my anxiety over Maggie had been replaced with the circumstantial mess and stress that my lovely wife had created. At least Nancy was rewarded with millions of dollars and her dream job: a license from the military to create weapons of mass destruction ... whereas Maggie would have to fight the urge, for the rest of her life, to use the drug that nearly killed her.

Jack called, saying he was worried about what Nancy might do next. With only a month before the big wedding, he was counting on me, his best man, to show up without any boils or viral diseases that my wife might be hatching in her laboratory. He reminded me how he'd warned me about her at the start: "Any woman that beautiful who can speak perfect English is trouble." And he hinted that maybe it would be for the best if Nancy didn't come to the wedding. I assured him that she had no interest in attending.

Chapter Thirty-Two

It's often said that the fear of an impending crisis is worse than the crisis itself. Well, like most everything else in my life lately, that maxim didn't apply.

Maggie gripped my hand tightly as the sirens roared. The ambulance was traveling at a great speed, twisting and turning like a boat rocked by unflinching waves. At any moment, I thought I was going to vomit all over Maggie, not that she would have noticed. She was in and out of consciousness, with an oxygen mask covering her mouth, and she was hooked up to an IV. The paramedic told me to try to keep her awake as he constantly monitored her vital signs. I kept pinching her ass really hard; with each pinch, her eyes opened wide like she was ready to kill me. Finally she was admitted into the Emergency Center at UCLA. I was told to stay in the waiting room and they would come talk to me once she was stable.

Earlier in the evening, I had been trying to get in touch with her. I knew her kids were at a sleepover, and I worried about her being alone all night. After repeatedly calling, I got in my car and drove to her house. The front door was unlocked. I walked straight up to her bedroom and found her passed out on the floor, her face in a puddle of vomit. Empty wine bottles and the drug of her undoing were scattered all over the place. At that moment, I wasn't even sure she was alive. I immediately called 911.

I turned Maggie over and rubbed my knuckles roughly over her sternum. She sat up, her eyes wide open like in some sick horror film, and she barfed all over me before flopping back down. I carried her into the bathroom and splashed cold water on her face as I waited for the sink to fill up. Then I dipped her head into the sink of cold water. That woke her up long enough to understand that help was on the way. As we waited for the ambulance, I dipped her head into the water every time she seemed to be nodding off, which was about every thirty seconds.

I tried to clean up in the hospital bathroom but I couldn't get rid of the stench. Soon the doctor came out and told me Maggie was sleeping comfortably and out of danger. He asked if she had previously attempted suicide, and I gave him a quick summary of how she had become addicted. He listened as if he had heard the same story a thousand times before.

I asked if I could see her, and he thought it would be best if I went home first and took a shower. She wasn't going anywhere.

I left Nancy a note on the bed explaining the situation since I had no way of reaching her at work. It was like she was in protective custody six days a week. I was tempted to call the general and ask when I should expect my wife back, but I already knew what he'd say: "She's working on a very important project, Joe. Surely you can understand the sensitive nature of such endeavors and the need for utmost secrecy. In the wrong hands, it could mean the end of civilization."

And I'd reply, "Haven't you figured out yet that she's insane on her best days and totally psychotic on her worst?"

And then he'd say, "She's not the first psycho we've hired. Most geniuses have emotional abnormalities. It's in their DNA."

Maggie was still asleep when I got back to the hospital. I had already arranged to have her return to the rehab center in Malibu. Since she was returning after only six months, she was allowed to have visitors after only two days and she was allowed one sleepover visitor (preferably a spouse, a longtime lover, or partner) once a week.

I bought a magazine in the gift shop, and the cover pictured an unlit cigarette. The caption read, "Are Tobacco Manufacturers on Life Support?" I turned to the article. It more or less summarized the last six months of congressional hearings into the hazardous effects of smoking. The Surgeon General and respected medical professionals throughout the country agreed that cigarettes were the contributing, if not the primary, cause of heart disease and cancer of the mouth, throat, and lungs. The nicotine in cigarettes was as addictive as heroin.

I started to laugh as I looked at pictures of concerned congressmen questioning tobacco executives. The sons of bitches were better actors than Olivier and Burton combined. In truth, every congressman on the committee received money from the very executives they were questioning. It was just a big show — a bargaining tool to extort even more money from Big Tobacco. In six months, the findings of the committee would be buried deep inside all the major newspapers throughout the country. The only journals and magazines that would give appropriate exposure and analysis to the recommendations and findings of the committee were medical and scientific publications — and who read them? Certainly not the sanitation worker addicted to three packs a day.

Maggie was awake when I walked back into her room. She looked so pale and fragile that I was at a loss for words. I sat on the bed beside her and took her hand.

"Pretty soon you're going to get tired of saving my life. What am I going to do then?" she asked. "At least this time I didn't bankrupt my family."

"Did you really try to kill yourself, Maggie? Or was it an accident? Remember our pledge to each other."

"I was craving the drug so much I tried to drown it out by drinking some wine, not the wisest choice. Two bottles later, I bought a bag of twenty pills. I was only going to take one, but one led to two and then three, and then I just swallowed a whole bunch, hoping I'd never wake up."

"During this entire episode, did you think at all of how difficult it would be for your kids to grow up without you? If something happened to you, don't you think that they might consider themselves somehow responsible for your actions? Did you once think of that?"

"They'd be much better off living with their father than with a junkie for a mother."

"And how about me, Maggie? Would I be so much better off without you in my life?"

"It would be a lot easier on your wallet," she said with a nervous laugh.

"When did you become so selfish?"

"Please, Joe, don't go there. I didn't ask for this."

I let go of her hand and placed my hands on her shoulders. "If you didn't look so frail, I would shake you so hard. Hopefully I could reawaken whatever brain cells were still alive in that head of yours."

She leaned back on the pillows and I took a seat in the chair. I flipped through the pages of the magazine and couldn't help seeing the connection between Maggie's situation and the millions of people addicted to cigarettes. Nancy was right. I was the conduit, the messenger, the street pimp pushing a deadly product. I rolled the magazine tightly and looked back at Maggie, then got up and held her tightly. I could hear her heart beating against my chest. "I love you so much ... so very much."

Chapter Thirty-Three

I left the hospital and drove directly to the office. It was just starting to get light outside, and at that moment I wasn't quite sure of anything.

The building seemed emptier than usual. The night watchman was asleep behind the lobby desk. As I got off the elevator and walked toward my office, the lights were on in Jack's office, but thankfully the door was closed. I entered my office and looked at the board outlining the ad campaign for the cigarette company — targeted groups of disadvantaged teens born with one foot already in the grave. It represented everything my parents would consider reprehensible, everything that would secure me a permanent place in hell. It was everything Nancy said it was. I was a pimp disguised in an expensive wardrobe and a fancy title.

I grabbed the board and smashed it repeatedly against the desk, then walked directly to Jack's door. I entered without knocking and found Jack at his desk drinking Russian vodka and smoking a cigar. He didn't seem at all surprised to see me. On the floor behind him were five young women asleep on mattresses. I doubted their combined ages reached the century mark. It was like a scene out of a World War II movie.

I sat down. "Jack, I want off the tobacco campaign."

"Why?"

"Do I need a reason after all this time? I want off and that's it!"

"Growing a conscience, are we, Joe? They insisted on you."

"They all insist on me."

"That's the price for being the best."

He poured me a glass of vodka. "Fine, you're off. They're nothing but a bunch of capitalistic leeches, anyway. I'll give it to someone else."

"Capitalistic leeches," I repeated, as I reached for my glass and shot down the vodka. Jack looked at me like Nancy would, like he was observing a lab rat.

"What's that on your chin?"

I looked at my reflection in the bottle of vodka. "Oh, I nicked myself shaving. What's the big deal?"

"You sure about that?"

"Of course I'm sure. What, you're afraid I'm sick with that virus?"

"Well, you are married to the deranged scientist who developed it."

I shook my head as he poured me another shot.

"Relax, Joe. Enjoy your life, because you never know what tomorrow might bring. My old man loved the ponies. He spent more time at the track than with his family. And he was the unluckiest man ever born. Couldn't pick the winner in a one-horse race. The last bet he ever made was on a hundred-to-one shot. After placing the bet, he took a few steps away from the booth and dropped dead of a heart attack. That winning ticket was enough to pay for his funeral."

I drove home and sat down at my desk. I took out the file for the tobacco campaign I kept at the house and started ripping it into pieces like a madman. I suddenly looked up, startled by Nancy, who was standing beside me.

"What are you doing here, Nancy?" I asked in a near panic. I had no idea how long she'd been there.

"I live here, and I'm married to the most loving and adorable man in the whole world. Besides, it's Sunday." She picked up the trashcan and held it as I dropped all the torn pieces and the rest of the file into the can. She took me by the hand and led me over to the couch. We sat down, and I lay my head on her lap as she ran her hands through my hair.

"When am I going to get you back?"

"Soon, Joe. Very soon."

"And do you think one day we might start a family?"

"Yes."

I fell asleep. When I woke up, Nancy was still there. After all, it was Sunday.

Chapter Thirty-Four

The con was simple. What was unusual was that Maggie was only twenty-nine. Most victims were middle-aged women, recently divorced, still hungry for attention, and very rich. The other thing was the brutality of the con, which left the victim not only financially ruined, but also addicted to a deadly drug.

The con artist, the gigolo, the engineer of the scheme, was usually a guy in his mid-thirties to early forties, very good-looking, superbly and expensively dressed, worldly, knowledgeable, and with an endearing and trusting personality. He came to a town like Los Angeles and rented a home in an affluent area such as Malibu, Bel-Air, or Beverly Hills. He leased a glamorous car like a Ferrari and selected a few high-class restaurants frequented by an elite clientele. He befriended a couple of waiters and bartenders, usually servers addicted to gambling and in constant need of extra money, and made it known that he was interested in a certain type of lady — a lonely divorcée, very rich, who drank and dined alone at the restaurant consistently a few times a week. He made it perfectly clear that he was willing to pay handsomely for information, and he always left great tips.

Maggie's routine after her second divorce was fairly consistent. On Mondays, Wednesdays, and Fridays, she visited a popular and fashionable restaurant in Brentwood after work. She usually sat at the bar, ordered a salad, two very expensive glasses of wine, and left great tips. Maggie was always talkative and social; no doubt the bartender knew more about her life than he needed to.

The bartender, a degenerate gambler, passed Maggie's routine information to the con artist. The con artist persuaded the bartender — for a mere $1000 — to drop a pill into Maggie's wine right at the time he appeared at the bar and made her acquaintance.

The bartender offered up this information — and the possible location of the con artist — right after both his hands were shattered by a baseball bat that made more contact with his hands than Ted Williams ever made with a baseball. He was then rewarded for his cooperation with a swift blow to the mouth with the butt of the bat. Needless to say, his bartender days were over and a pair of false teeth were certainly in his future if he could possibly afford such a luxury.

The drug gave Maggie a sense of euphoria, and instead of staying only for her usual two glasses of wine and departing, she stuck around until closing, talking to the con artist. They made a date for the following night, same place, same time, and so started the con, Maggie's addiction to the deadly drug, and her financial ruin.

After successfully siphoning off the victim's assets, a con artist typically would skip town, but this piece of shit got greedy and instead simply relocated to a zip code only a few miles away. After all, no city in the country has a greater abundance of profitable targets — lonely, rich ladies — than the city of Los Angeles.

The former bartender's information was invaluable. Late one night, as the con artist was escorting another target up the stairs to his newly rented Malibu home, the car alarm on his newly rented Porsche went off. Being a gentleman, he let the lady into the house and went back down to check on the car. As he unsuccessfully tried to shut the alarm off, the two gentlemen who had visited the bartender came strolling by, and with one swift swing of the same baseball bat to the car's dashboard, the alarm instantly went quiet.

The piece of shit was dragged behind a bunch of bushes and had his face rearranged, tongue removed, genitals forever made useless, and knees broken in such a way to cripple him for the rest of his life.

As if that wasn't bad enough, in the hospital the son of a bitch was booked on possession of drugs with intent to sell, blackmail, grand larceny, fraud, and possession of illegal firearms. If he had any desire left to see freedom and the light of day again, he would never have the opportunity after being convicted on all these charges.

I insisted on Maggie assigning me power of attorney over her estate and appointing me her guardian. Usually it's a husband or relative, but I was the closest thing she had to either one. She would not be allowed to leave the Malibu Rehab Center until I felt comfortable with the state of her recovery and consented to her release. I had to come up with a plan to help her resist inevitable temptation, even if it meant that she, the children, and their nanny had to move into my house. For now, with her safely tucked away in Malibu, I had some time to think of a solution that wouldn't cost Maggie her life at the hands of Nancy and would maybe also spare me whatever was left of my manhood.

Chapter Thirty-Five

When Nancy first told me that I would be getting her back soon, I was overjoyed. Then I remembered that in Nancy's mind "very soon" might mean ten years because, in the history of the planet, ten years was little more than a blip.

Just a few days ago, she handed me a stack of paychecks, forty-four to be exact, that she hadn't cashed since starting work for the Department of Defense. She asked me to deposit them into our account, and when I told her that most checks needed to be cashed within ninety days, she replied, "Nonsense, they're marked DOD. It's not like they're going out of business." The total amount, after taxes, came to $67,000, and she was right — the bank had no problem depositing the checks.

Just over a year ago, Nancy had been three months behind in her rent. Now she was worth millions, and her carefree attitude toward money hadn't changed. It was baffling to me that a woman who believed that mathematics was the one pure science that explained everything could not — or refused to — keep track of her own money. Since getting married, she had not once withdrawn money from any of our accounts, and I was quite sure she had never checked how much she was worth. She ridiculed me for not buying her a new computer for the house and her own car, but never once did she threaten to go to the bank and simply take out the money and buy these things for herself.

Maggie's new visitor policy at the rehab center was convenient for me. No more sneaking in the back way, and certainly it helped her recovery to see her children every day, along with other visitors I trusted to be supportive and helpful. Since I didn't have a wife to go home to after work, I drove out there and visited Maggie five nights a week. George visited in the mornings after driving Jack and his entourage around all night. The children and the nanny visited after school, so she had several guests each day and no chance to feel unloved, forgotten, or left behind. Between us we made sure Maggie knew she had a life to come home to once she was well and ready.

After three weeks, I ran into George there on a Friday night. I didn't think anything of it. He told me Jack didn't need him that night; he and his entourage had decided to order in and stay in the office.

The three of us talked for a number of hours and when I was about to leave, I asked George if he wanted to walk out with me. It was getting late and Maggie looked tired. He told me that he was Maggie's overnight guest, and, as I was trying to process this piece of information, Maggie said, "And we're planning on getting married, so it's time to relinquish your power of attorney and guardianship over me."

"I don't think so, Maggie. I'll do that on the day the two of you get married."

George remained silent as Maggie remarked, "You really have lost all faith in me."

"No! It's just that you mean so much to me that I refuse to take any chances with your well-being. I couldn't be happier for the two of you. It's the best news I've heard in a long time." I shook George's hand and congratulated him, then kissed Maggie on the cheek and whispered, "This is a very wise choice. I am really proud of you."

Three days later, George and Maggie were married at the Malibu Rehab Center. Before getting into my car after the ceremony, I turned one last time and looked at the beautiful bride, who smiled back as she reached down and touched the crucifix around her neck.

I opened the door to my house and was greeted by my gorgeous wife, who threw her arms around me and kissed me for what seemed like a blissful eternity. She was now all mine, like she had promised. In two weeks, she was invited to the White House where the President of the United States was going to award her with a medal — in a private ceremony — for her outstanding and notable service to our country.

It was an amazing amount of good news to process in a short time. Maggie married to the one man I knew had always been in love with her. I knew George would look after her and protect her from herself. He could handle any outside forces that might pose a threat. Now I could focus my full attention on my Nancy, who was finally free after being a guest of the military for nearly a year. I was sure the whole thing about receiving a medal from the President had to be a joke until I remembered that Nancy did not lie — a fact she had proven time and time again.

Since she was going to be free, I asked Nancy if she might reconsider going to Jack's wedding in a week. After all, I was the best man and didn't have a date. She laughed and whispered, "I still have samples of the boil virus. You wouldn't want your boss spending his honeymoon in the hospital with prolonged paralysis to his genitals ... As for you, my darling, I have faith that you will behave properly, and, although I will miss you dearly, I'm confident that you will be home at a reasonable hour."

It would be an understatement to say that Jack's wedding was unusual. The bride was dressed in traditional Russian attire. She wore a white Kokoshnik headdress and veil, and her gown was made of white satin adorned with gold silk roses. The five bridesmaids and maid of honor wore similar gowns but no headdresses or veils.

Jack, not to be outdone, wore a gaudy robe, which did nothing to hide his bulging stomach, and a lewd and bedazzling silk overcoat that, if I didn't know better, I would have thought he'd stolen off the body of Peter the Great. I wore a traditional black tuxedo.

After the lengthy church ceremony, we were driven to one of Jack's former wives' home. She was currently out of town and kind enough to let Jack hold the reception there. The house had ten bedrooms, which was convenient because the maid of honor and bridesmaids were deftly mixing business with wedding bliss.

There were 200 guests, including Maggie's fan club, who were disappointed that Maggie couldn't make the gala reception. I lessened their disappointment by paying for the first round of bridesmaids.

I gave the same speech that I had given at Jack's previous wedding, adding a few Russian phrases for effect. Jack started to cry as he stood up and hugged me like a big teddy bear. It was quite touching, but, when he wouldn't let go, it became uncomfortable. Eventually his bride pulled him away, sat him down, and patted him on the head. I was quietly grateful.

I snuck out the back way and paid one of the chauffeurs $200 to drive me home. I walked into the bedroom before midnight and looked down at Nancy under the covers reading a book. She pulled back the sheets to reveal her red lingerie. She tied the red bandanna around her head and with her finger motioned for me to join her.

"I've been waiting so patiently," she said in a sultry voice.

"Sorry to keep you waiting." I ripped the stupid tuxedo off and joined my better half.

Chapter Thirty-Six

It was a beautiful day in Washington, DC. After going through a detailed security check at the White House, my wife was ushered into a private room while I was escorted to a folding chair in the Rose Garden. There was a podium and about ten chairs in a single row thirty feet in front of it. The photographer was busy setting up. No press was allowed. This was a private ceremony.

Suddenly, I went flying out of my chair as General Pierce came up behind me and slapped me on the back. He laughed as he helped me to my feet. "You need to work on your upper body, Joe."

He sat down beside me and continued, "Your wife insisted that you be invited. She's a real asset to our country, a true patriot."

"That much I can guarantee you, sir. She's one in a million."

"Damn right, she is." The general reached into his pocket and pulled out a flask. He took a swig and pointed to the initials carved into the leather exterior. "T.R.JR." He proudly said, "Theodore Roosevelt, Jr.! You know who that was?"

"President Teddy Roosevelt's son."

"That's right, Joe. I doubt there are a thousand people in our country who know about his amazing contributions to our nation. A true hero — a Medal of Honor recipient, like his famous father — fought in both world wars. The only general on D-Day to land on the beaches with his troops, at the age of fifty-six, with the help of a cane."

He handed me the flask. At first I was hesitant to take a sip, and then I decided that if I wanted to survive this conversation without any major injuries, I better take a long and honorable swig. "Smooth."

"Johnnie Walker Blue, only the best." The general took another swig and handed the flask back to me. Who was I to refuse?

"Ever miss the excitement of combat?"

"Yeah, like I miss a swift kick to the balls." He stood up and looked at an arriving group of other high-ranking military personnel. "And now I have to go socialize with a bunch of armchair generals," he said with a bit of disdain.

I shook the general's hand. "We'll be in touch, Joe." He walked toward the other brass.

I sat back down and thought how wonderful it was that the general had my wife's back, even if it meant eliminating me. The President made a short but touching speech and then was handed the medal, which was attached to a red, white and blue ribbon that he tied behind my beautiful and brilliant wife's neck. We all stood and clapped as a Secret Service agent tapped me on the shoulder. "The President would like to speak to you. Please follow."

I looked over at Nancy, whose eyes caught a glimpse of me walking away. It felt like I was moving a thousand miles away from her with each step I took in the direction of the agent. I was escorted to a side room and was told that the President would be in shortly. In the meantime, the chief of staff entered and briefed me on the context of the meeting. The president wanted to know if I would be interested in running his west coast re-election campaign.

The president entered a few minutes later.

After leaving the White House, Nancy and I went sightseeing around the city. She hung on to me in a way she had never done in public. She wrapped her arms around my left arm and rested her head on my shoulder. She barely spoke; even before some of the most magnificent monuments in the world, she made very few observations — this from a woman who had a hundred things to say about the placement of an apple on the kitchen table.

Back at the hotel, I watched Nancy get ready. We had a reservation at the finest restaurant in the city. She was dressed in a white slip, sitting before a mirror putting on makeup and fixing her hair. I walked up behind her and rubbed her shoulders. "The President wanted to know if I'd run his west coast re-election campaign. I told him it would be an honor, but my calendar was filled with a major project that I couldn't abandon or delay under any circumstances."

"You told him no?" Nancy was shocked.

"I told him that because the project I'm working on is the most important thing in my life — being the best husband I can be to the most wonderful and beautiful wife in the world."

Nancy started to cry, and I handed her a few tissues. "And what does the general want you working on next?"

She shook her head and replied, "I told them that we planned on starting a family and I wouldn't be available for quite a while. The general comes off as a tough guy, but deep down he's a real pushover."

She stood up, threw her arms around me, and held on tightly. "I love you so much, Joe."

We canceled our reservation at the restaurant.

Chapter Thirty-Seven

It's hard to say why a dream you've been having for years suddenly changes as though it's been edited like a film, but that's exactly what happened. For the most part, it stayed the same up to the point where my prick of a lawyer, in a hurry to get to some living customers, drops my coffin off by my parents' grave and the cemetery police gather around and start singing "La Marseillaise" from the movie *Casablanca*. Ilsa, the beautiful Ingrid Bergman, suddenly appears beside me, and as I go to kiss her, she changes into the even more beautiful girl of my dreams, Nancy. Edgar Allan Poe's "Annabel Lee" comes to mind: "My darling, my darling, my life and my bride."

We kiss passionately as the lid of the coffin springs open, and as we walk toward my parents' graves, the cemetery police stop singing and start enthusiastically clapping. We look down at my parents' names engraved on the tombstone, and directly below are our own names, mine and Nancy's, with only our birth dates present … the rest to be filled in much later.

Instead of walking over the Whitestone Bridge, we find ourselves walking over the Brooklyn Bridge from the Manhattan side. Nancy holds my hand as she gives me a tutorial on the building of this magnificent structure. The chief engineer, Washington Roebling, was a genius. The soaring towers on each side of the bridge are monumental achievements that stand up against anything built before or since. The mathematical precision, alignment of the cables, and the stiffness built into the surface of the bridge are still to this day, 150 years later, the blueprint used for building many suspension bridges.

The bridge is empty except for the two of us. The sun is just starting to rise as the sound of a trumpet can be heard in the distance. I look away from Nancy, and there is Louis Armstrong (Satchmo), walking down the middle of the bridge, playing his horn with a band of musicians following him. He is singing "What a Wonderful World." As I turn back toward Nancy, I feel an overabundance of joy and happiness, and then I wake up, humming the tune.

Acknowledgments

To Teresita Ann, a beautiful addition to the family.

To Cagney, a life way too short, but a source of great happiness and inspiration.

And to Iguana Books and its wonderful and talented staff.

CPSIA information can be obtained
at www.ICGtesting.com
Printed in the USA
BVHW03s0147230818
525329BV00001BA/28/P